The Silence

Linda Tweedie
Kate McGregor

Published by Fledgling Press 2015

www.fledglingpress.co.uk

ISBN 9781905916993

Acknowledgements

This book was written in collaboration with Kate McGregor, without whose input it would have been an entirely different publication (a leaflet maybe!) Because if she couldn't cross her i's and dot her t's, this book would still be languishing somewhere as an untitled Word document, never to be read.

Next it has to be Clare from Fledgling Press, who not only believed in us, but had to put up with two loud, overbearing women, who always know best, even when they don't, and who send her schedule into the stratosphere.

Thanks to Graeme who always knows what we want, especially as we never know ourselves – now that's smart.

Finally to my husband, David, who has the nous to keep out of the way, not to ask stupid questions and has learned after all these years how to work the dishwasher and washing machine. Shame he doesn't know which is which . . .

Well done and thanks.

Linda and Kate

CATHIE MCGREGOR 1938 – 2014
This one's for you.

The little girl in the white dress was crying. She was crying for her da and the white dress was turning red, blood red.

The Party

The music could be heard three streets away; no-one could remember there ever being a street party like this. You had to hand it to Big Paddy. By God, he did things in style. Enough booze to sink the Titanic and table upon table of magnificent food, all probably supplied free gratis to the Big Man. Very few shopkeepers would fail to take the opportunity of impressing Big Paddy Coyle and getting into his good books. What was a bit of food or a few bottles, compared to being in favour or showing respect? No, you wouldn't want to be out of favour with the Coyles. Let's face it, the recipients of his generosity couldn't give a shit whether it was paid for or not, as long as it was free to them.

Paddy's mother Lizzie was dressed to the nines and not from the Barra's either – straight from Marks and Spencer in Argyle Street no less. She was over the moon that he and Bridget had decided to hold the celebration here in the family home, and not over at that posh gaff, as she called their beautiful villa on the outskirts of the city. She was in her element, holding court on the strip of grass she lovingly called her garden; home to a few scrawny geraniums and an old, chipped, garishly-painted gnome. She was queen of all she surveyed thanks to her boys, especially her eldest, Patrick Joseph Coyle, but it hadn't always been that way.

"Great party, Paddy," called one of the guests as Paddy passed by.

"Aye, grand, lad," his neighbour agreed. They were like the two old codgers off the Muppets, thought Paddy, smiling.

Where was she? He scanned the party area, searching for his wife, Bridget. Spying her alongside his ma he made his way across the green, through the crowds of well-wishers, towards them.

They weren't going to take what he had to tell them well, but he had no choice. The world didn't stop because Paddy Coyle was throwing a party.

"My God, I'm stuffed," laughed Teresa, his mother's neighbour and confidant. "Jesus, you outdid yourself this time, Paddy me boy, it'll take a large dose of castor oil to shift this lot," as she patted her distended abdomen and gave rip to an extremely loud fart.

"My God, Teresa, have a bit of decorum," scolded Lizzie. "Jesus, the priests are just over there."

"Och, they wouldn't hear it from way over there," smirked the culprit.

"No, but they'll feckin' well smell it, you rank old biddy," laughed the matriarch.

"You never change," said Paddy, "make sure you take a bit of grub away with you, and a drink for himself." Teresa's husband, Peter, had been bed-ridden for years after an accident at work. Everyone knew it was for the 'comp' and there was sod all wrong with him, he was just a lazy bastard, but Teresa wouldn't have a word said against him, despite the fact he was the most miserable, cantankerous old git Paddy had ever met. But Teresa was his mother's best mate and many times over the years the Coyles had been 'helped out' and Paddy would never forget that.

"Can I have a word? Excuse us a minute, Teresa. Glad you're enjoying yourself."

He led his mother and wife back into the terraced house. The house Lizzie had lived in for the past thirty years. The one in which she'd given birth to her three sons and that she-devil of a daughter, Marie. Who, incidentally, was the only member of the family missing from the celebrations. No doubt the prodigal daughter would come rolling home in last night's clothes, stinking of last night's booze and last night's man.

There was no reasoning with the girl. She went her own way, doing her own thing, regardless of how much shame she brought on her mother and her brothers, and there was plenty of shame at that. The latest being snugly wrapped and fast asleep in the stylish Silver Cross pram, bought, of course, by

Paddy, there being no husband or father to stump up. Only the colour of the wee mite gave a clue as to his parentage and neither of those gentlemen were likely to step up to the plate. Coincidentally, they had both been reported missing. Despite that, the house was always a haven for her family, no matter what trouble they might be in.

Oh, she had no illusions about her sons. Under the façade of 'successful businessmen' Lizzie knew well what her Patrick and his brothers got up to, and whether she approved or not, they were her boys and she would always stand by them. It was that 'business' that kept her in the style she had now become accustomed to. Her sons were good to their mother, nothing but the best, and Lizzie knew that. Marie, too, had a lot to be thankful for, but needless to say she wasn't.

The first thing that struck a visitor upon entering 28 Lomond Gardens was the sparkle. The place shone like a new pin and always smelled of polish and bleach. Paddy was sure his mother used Pledge as an air freshener, and it wasn't the first time he'd walked into a cloud of polish and almost choked.

"Okay, what's up?" queried Lizzie. "Surely whatever it is can wait till tomorrow, lad. Can we not have this day without any shenanigans?"

"I'm sorry, Ma, but I have to leave. There's a problem at the warehouse and the polis are all over the place. We have to go."

Although disappointed, Lizzie sighed in agreement, business was business and he had to go. But not so Bridget, she wasn't having any of it. It was seldom she argued back with Paddy, always giving him his place and honestly, in her heart she knew that he wouldn't leave Erin's party unless it was absolutely necessary. But she certainly wasn't going to make it easy for him

"*We* have to go?" queried his wife. "And who are this *we*? Surely, if the boys are going they can handle it without you holding their hands?"

"For fuck's sake, Bridget, you know the score," said her exasperated husband. "I've no time for this."

"Make bloody time," snapped Bridget. "And I know the score alright, but no, Paddy, send the others. This is your only daughter's first holy communion and nothing, I mean *nothing*, should interfere with today."

"I have to, Bridget. You know I wouldn't go if I could help it, but I must." Paddy had that steel glint in his eye which brooked no arguments and Bridget, angry though she was, knew not to push her luck. "Now, be a good girl and make sure everyone is enjoying themselves and I'll be as quick as I can. You won't even notice I've gone."

Bridget was furious. Since the day they were married, at every party, wedding and funeral they had ever attended Paddy had left her on her own at some point, to go and attend to 'business'. Well, it would be a long time before she let him off with this one.

In fairness to her man, he worked relentlessly for

his family and Bridget was well aware that she and Erin came first in Paddy's life and he would willingly die for them. The only real disappointment in their lives was that there were no brothers or sisters for their precious little girl. For the first few years she had been frantic and the disappointment every month was hard to bear, but as time went on she resigned herself to the situation and channelled all her love and affection on the two most important beings in her life. She kept the magnificent home perfect, tended to her daughter's and husband's needs and was on call to any member of the family who needed help. She was a diamond and everybody loved Bridget, none more so than her husband even when she was being a stubborn mare.

The party was in full swing; there were pony rides, courtesy of a couple of traveller boys who Paddy had helped out recently. The kids' magician, with the expensive coke habit, was busy churning out balloon animals, each one with its own little white moustache, just like the man making them. The DJ was blasting out the latest Madonna hit and the green was awash with little mini brides, all prancing about in their finest, and dozens of not-so-white-clad little lads having a whale of a time. The makeshift bar was three deep and the two volunteers were doing a roaring trade. Free booze was a luxury few, if any, had enjoyed before and there would be a few sair heids in the morning, including the two Fathers.

Father Jack was Craigloch's parish priest. It was once a thriving community, but like many big housing estates, most of its inhabitants were living way below the poverty line. As the more fortunate families were rehoused and moved away, the empty houses soon became squats and the scheme was riddled with junkies and crackheads.

As far as Father Jack was concerned the Coyles were a good Catholic family and could do no wrong. No matter what rumours or stories circulated, the donations from Paddy and the brothers far outweighed any gossip.

The Coyles were all regular churchgoers, apart from Marie of course, but Lizzie was up and out to first mass most mornings, often accompanied by Patrick. Whether he was on his way to work or coming home was not for Father Jack to speculate, especially as there was always a fifty pound note in the collection plate.

Canon O'Farrell, on the other hand, didn't share Father Jack's views on the Coyle family. Lizzie was a good woman, but the others were scum of the earth, devil's spawn and a few other adjectives to boot. He especially loathed Patrick with a passion. Oh, he would accept his hospitality and all the benefits that came with having such a powerful family in the parish, but it was his God-given mission to destroy the man and destroy him he would. And that day was nigh.

The cut ran deep within the canon and went back many years, to a time when, as a young priest, he first landed in Glasgow. Way before the present turf wars started. The 'Ice Cream Wars'. He laughed at the absurdity. Only a place like this could come up with such an idiotic name, and he knew, as God would be his judge, that Paddy Coyle was at the centre of the feud and that the 'Big Man' would stop at nothing until he controlled the east of the city.

The two priests hated a drink or two – between the pair of them the Fathers had demolished a bottle of single malt whisky, washed down with more than a few pints of the black stuff.

It was perhaps time to make a move back to the parish house before the early evening mass. Not that he expected many of their parishioners to attend, they were all too busy enjoying themselves, courtesy of the Coyles.

"Shite," muttered Father Jack, knowing full well he would be the one who volunteered to do his duty.

The fly auld bugger did little or no parish work nowadays and conducted even fewer masses. He spent most of his time with the young trainees who had been assigned to St. Jude's and of late, a less Christian or devout bunch of scoundrels he had yet to meet.

Father Jack had his own views on what was going on in his parish, but better to keep his own counsel, for the moment anyway. So there was no chance, given the amount of booze he'd consumed, that Canon O'Farrell would officiate tonight.

Zig-zagging across the green on their way home, being stopped every couple of yards by either the recipient of the holy sacrament or the parents of such, they eventually reached the end of the avenue just as one of Big Paddy's ice cream vans came trundling into view, the chimes blaring above the cacophony of the DJ. The ears of every kid in the vicinity pricked up.

There's nothing a kid loves more than ice cream, mused Father Jack. The only thing to top that was free ice cream. Heaven had just arrived, playing *Popeye the Sailor Man,* and even before the van had stopped there was a healthy queue.

Clinging on to her mother's skirt, "Please, Mum, please just ask him," pleaded Erin. "Please. My da would let me, and it's his van anyway. Go on, Mum, ask him."

To be fair, Erin Coyle seldom asked for privileges and she was right, her da would have given in immediately. The van was, after all, one of his fleet.

"Okay, since you've been such a good girl I'll ask. Mind, he might say no, health and safety and all that."

Bridget walked up to the open window and motioned to Jamesie that she wanted a word.

"Jamesie, I won't be annoyed if you say no, but Erin's desperate to have a wee go at serving. Would you let her? It's not as if you're selling the stuff and Paddy will be good for anything she messes, what do you say?"

Hey! There was no way he would ever be likely to refuse a request from Bridget Coyle. If the girl blew the van up he would still take the blame. Jamesie Flynn had only recently fallen heir to his own van, the previous incumbent having disappeared after the third attempt on his life had proved one attempt too many.

The vans were notorious throughout the country. They were used as cover to sell drugs, carry stolen goods, a depository for weapons. In fact, the vans sold everything except ice cream, or very little. It was a dangerous occupation and the average lifespan of a van man was not long. Not only were they constantly targeted by other outfits, but the filth raided them with such regularity they were known locally as the 'Serious Chime Squad'. But Jamesie had no such fears – having ridden shotgun on nearly every van in the Coyle fleet he knew the score and what to look out for, or so he thought.

Okay, maybe his wasn't the most lucrative round on the patch, but it was a start and Jamesie had plans. He was an ambitious young lad and meant to go places, not like most of the other drivers. No way would he shove the profits up his nose. No, as far as he was concerned drugs were for the punters, not him.

He couldn't believe his luck when the Big Man himself had approached him about taking over the round. He had worked his way up the ranks, quietly and efficiently, getting whatever job done with no fuss and, more to the point, no come-back. So he wouldn't ever qualify as one of the heavies, but he took shit from no-one and could more than hold his own, he would do alright.

Certainly, bringing free ice cream to Erin Coyle's

party was a stroke of genius and the big man wouldn't forget such a gesture. More brownie points.

"Of course she can. Come away in, poppet, but mind your dress, this is messy work."

"Look, ten minutes and I'll come back for her. That should be long enough for boredom to set in," smiled Bridget. "Erin, you be a good girl and listen to what Jamesie says. I'll be over with nanny."

"Oh Lord, look at what the cat's dragged in," Bridget muttered to herself, spying her young sister-in-law, Marie, staggering into the street.

Even in such a state Marie Coyle was a stunner. She had long, dark titian hair, green eyes and the almost translucent skin of the pure Celt, a figure to die for and a mouth like an Irish navvy. Marie, waving furiously to Bridget, turned, pulled her ridiculously short skirt even higher and wiggled her bare arse for all to see.

Bridget almost collapsed with laughter. She loved the mad devil, but she was so thankful that the brothers had gone off on their mission or there would have been murder. Lizzie, on the other hand, looked like a bulldog chewing a wasp, and even in her befuddled state Marie knew to avoid her mother for the moment.

"Hey, kiddo, what are you doing in there? Is your da so skint he's got you out working to pay for this lot?" she joked with her niece. Marie was great with everyone else's kids, just not her own.

"Have a cornet, Auntie Marie. Go on, pick any flavour, I can do them all, honest. Sprinkles, flakes, any topping."

"Surprise me, darling, surprise me."

Erin was in her element and working the whipped ice machine was just so cool. Of course, her Auntie Marie got the works – toppings and sauces.

As she turned back to the serving window, holding an absolute masterpiece, the youngster was puzzled. Where was her auntie? In Marie's place there was a man, a man wearing a mask. Was somebody playing a trick? The man had a gun.

No-one had paid any attention to the car that had pulled up behind the van, not until the three men emerged, all with shotguns, all wearing balaclavas. First there was a shot through the windscreen. Next the back door was blown off its hinges and finally the interior took the remainder of the shots. Only the chimes survived.

Her dress, oh, look at her lovely dress. Had she spilled something on it? The red stain was getting bigger. People were screaming. Where was Auntie Marie? What was wrong with Jamesie? Father Jack had fallen down; everything was strange. She wanted her da. Where was her da?

Canon O'Farrell was the only person not taken by surprise.

The Raid

Although loathe to leave the party, Paddy made off with his twin brothers, Sean and Michael, in one car and wee Davie and Mark in another. The rest of the boys, most of whom had enjoyed the free bar, were scrabbling about looking for lifts.

The Coyles, being a close-knit family, always had each other's backs. But physically and temperamentally they were as different as chalk and cheese.

Patrick, the eldest, stood at 6'2" and was as broad as he was tall. He was a handsome devil who exuded dominance and no-one ever disputed his authority. He was well named 'The Big Man'.

'The Twins', as they were always referred to, had the stocky build of the typical Glaswegian. At 5'10", whilst certainly not small, they were dwarfed by their older brother. Like most identical twins they seemed to be joined at the hip.

Michael was the quieter of the two, the thinker. He

was a wizard with figures and was the number man of the firm. He could calculate to the nearest pound what any business should be taking, and heaven help the man who said otherwise.

Sean was the party animal; he knew where everything was happening, the latest 'in-places' and who was selling what in every club. It seemed like he spent his time chasing skirt and having a good time, but he missed nothing and whatever situations he did get into with irate husbands or boyfriends, he simply blamed them on his brother. Only their mother, sister and Paddy could actually tell them apart. Together, the family ran the East End of Glasgow – pubs, clubs, saunas and vans. They were a force to be reckoned with.

The Coyle boys, like most of their contemporaries, had had a hard upbringing and learned the rules of the street before they could walk. Their father, Seamus, was a handsome genial seaman, often absent for months on end. Money was sporadic and haphazard which meant Lizzie and the boys continually lived on the edge. Eventually, lo and behold, the wanderer would return and it would be the land of milk and honey, but only for a while.

Every night was party night for Seamus; the house was full of food, drink and hangers-on. He would hold court with tales of his adventures which almost always involved being drunk and stuck in foreign prisons. Everyone loved the bones of him. He was great company and would give a body his last penny. But it was hard for Lizzie to watch the stupid arse buy his popularity. The money being squandered could keep her and his sons for months.

The man was generous to a fault, but when Seamus had drunk and gambled what little there was, the wanderlust would once again grab him. Full of promises to send money every week and to sign on for shorter trips, the family waved him off, hearing the same old promises and knowing he had no real thought for his family or how they would cope until his next leave.

On his last trip to the Far East he had simply failed to report for duty and had never been seen or heard of since. The consensus of opinion was that he'd been drunk and fallen overboard or, like one of the tales he spun, he was being held captive in some far-off jail. Either one, without proof, meant the shipping company would not pay out any compensation or insurance money, which meant the family found themselves in an even worse financial crisis than usual and, yet again, left to struggle in the proverbial . . .

Life had been desperate, to say the least. There was no money coming in and a new baby was on the way – a parting gift from Seamus' last home visit. No food in the house, no coal for a fire and they were reduced to burning what few sticks of furniture they had left. Lizzie had exhausted all channels of help. So, at the tender age of fourteen, it fell to Paddy to feed the family. He took any job he could. He worked from early morning, delivering milk, then on to delivering bags of coal and logs for the local fuel merchant.

Few grown men could carry the hundredweight bags, but these were nothing to the big lad. He would toss them over his shoulder as though they were full of feathers and easily run up four flights of stairs.

To top his week off he acted as a bookie's runner on a Saturday. It was this job that taught Paddy a valuable lesson, and one he never forgot – gambling was the curse of the working man. In the first few weeks of working for 'Bent Harry', the turf accountant, he listened to all the tales of glory. Men who had never had more than a fiver to spare would win hundreds, sometimes thousands, but forgot about the thousands they had lost over the years.

"If Shenanigan's Lad had come in at 50:1, I'd have 100K."

"Put your shirt on Pure Dead Cert, he can't lose."

"Got it from the horse's mouth."

Three weeks on the trot he went home with nothing. Listening to the get-rich-quick promises, and having gambled all of what he earned, Paddy Coyle never placed another bet in his life.

Between his wages and tips, the young lad probably earned nearly as much as the average man twice his age, and while they were not living in the lap of luxury he managed to keep a roof over their heads and put food on the table, but there was nothing left over for extras.

Even at such a tender age Paddy promised himself that life wouldn't always be like this. One day he'd make his mark, one day there would be money to spare. He had no idea how he would do it, but he knew it would be so.

He had virtually given up on schooling. It didn't seem to be acceptable for him to turn up as black as the Earl of Hell's waistcoat and continually falling asleep in class was not tolerated. Patrick Coyle was not a popular pupil with the teaching staff of St. Jude's Secondary School. One nun in particular, Sister Mary-Claire, seemed to have it in for the young lad and took demonic delight in drawing attention to his dirty, ragged clothes and embarrassing him in front of his classmates. Paddy hated her.

Between her and Father O'Farrell they made his school life a misery. Any misdemeanours merited outrageous punishment and on many occasions Paddy's hands were bleeding and cut through excessive use of the cane.

Such treatment was commonplace in the school, but no-one ever dreamed of complaining. Most parents would take the stance that Junior had more than likely done something to merit the punishment. After all, the perpetrators were reckoned to be devoted to doing good. Patrick Coyle would never admit to being in pain, not even to God.

His reputation was passed on to the twins. Although they were devils and spent most of the day disrupting their class, much to the amusement and delight of their classmates, they were just lads full of mischief and certainly didn't merit the punishments meted out to them. The sins of the brother (not the father) certainly seemed to be visiting them. The fact that they were identical meant no-one was ever sure who had actually carried out the crimes. The solution to this was simply to punish both. School was not a happy place for any of the Coyle boys and they couldn't wait to get away.

The final straw for Paddy came towards the end of the summer term. The twins, as usual, had been up to some dodge or other and had been sent to 'The Office' to be dealt with. There was nothing unusual in that, they were frequent visitors to the Head's office. However, it wasn't the genial Canon O'Brian who was in residence that day, but Father O'Farrell, newly arrived from Galway. Determined to tighten up St Jude's and maintain discipline, Father O'Farrell was a great believer in corporal punishment.

Paddy heard the yells from the other side of the school yard and knew immediately his brothers were in trouble. He crashed his way into the office and was met with the sight of his two eleven-year-old brothers, bare-arsed, being thrashed by this manic priest.

Paddy grabbed the switch from the priest and exacted his own extreme punishment on the quivering coward. The twins and Sister Mary-Claire had to wrestle the cane from him, fearing that Paddy would do serious damage.

Paddy Coyle had just made his first real enemy, as had Father Francis O'Farrell. Standing over the priest, Paddy bent down and whispered into his battered face. "If you ever touch one of mine again, they'll not be able to stop me. I will send you to your maker, whoever that might be."

Paddy instantly became an urban legend and

Father O'Farrell was hated by every kid in the neighbourhood.

The Journey

Despite the urgency, Michael drove through the city streets sedately, never exceeding the speed limit. No point in drawing attention to themselves or getting a tug for driving like the Dukes of Hazard. As they neared the quayside, expecting to be swamped by flashing blue lights, there was no-one around, only one old codger walking his dog.

"What the fuck's going on?" yelled Paddy as the 4 x 4 screeched to a halt. The warehouse and loading bay were deserted. The watchman, George, who'd been with the Coyles for years, jumped to attention.

"Afternoon, boys. Don't often see you on a Sunday," said the old chap, hurriedly shoving the Sunday papers under the desk.

"What's happened, George? Where are they all? What did they take?"

"Sorry, who took what, boss?" puzzled the watchman. "I've not seen a soul since I came in at six this morning."

"The polis," said an irritated Paddy, now surrounded by the most sober of the partygoers.

"You called me, you senile old bastard. You said the place was fucking teeming with filth and they were demanding entry."

"No' me, son. I never phoned you. I never phoned anybody. Why would I? It's been like a grave here."

"What the fuck's going on?" asked Michael.

"This old cunt's gone senile," roared Paddy. "He's saying he never phoned me, and I've dragged everyone down here and fallen out with the missus for a joke. I'll fuckin' joke him."

"Hold it, Paddy," interrupted Michael. "This is George you're talking about. Tell me what happened."

"What the fuck do you mean tell you what happened? Do you think it's me that's fucking senile, is that what you're saying?"

"No," said Michael. "Just tell me the story. Who phoned and what did they say?"

"That stupid old bastard phoned me. He said, Paddy, it's George. You better get here quick, there's big trouble. The polis are all over the place and demanding entry to the warehouse."

"Sorry! Again, what did the person say?"

"Jesus. How many fucking times? Hello, Paddy . . ."

"Hang on there," Michael laid his hand on Paddy's arm. "George never calls you Paddy."

"What does he call me, fucking Irene?" asked an irate Paddy.

"He calls you Boss, always has. I have never

21

heard George call anyone by their name. He calls me number one twin and Sean baby twin, ever since we were kids."

"What the fuck does it matter what the stupid old bastard called me? He told me the place was crawling with . . ."

The conversation was interrupted by the roar of a powerful vehicle, speeding up the quayside, blasting the horn and flashing its lights. As it drew abreast of the Coyle clan, a figure rolled down the passenger window and threw out a scrap of bloodstained material before speeding off.

"What the fuck!" Diving to retrieve the article Paddy shouted, "Get back! Get back to the party now!"

Background

"Jump Paddy, jump, it's safe" called Pete. "C'mon, the polis will be here any minute. Jump, ya big bastard."

Pete McClelland was doubled in two, laughing at his accomplice's predicament. Somehow Paddy's ragged jeans had snagged on a branch and he was caught fast in the tree blocking their escape route. His only chance was to remove the offending articles and go commando.

"Throw me the goods, Paddy," called Pete, well aware of how close they were to being caught.

"Shit, there's some fucker coming." Throwing the bag down to his pal, Paddy turned to face the music. Pete was off, no way was he hanging about, and it was every man for his own.

Two burly Glasgow policemen with a huge, slavering Alsatian had reached Paddy, who had wriggled out of his jeans which were now being savaged by the brute. Paddy was about to crash bare-arsed into the arms of the law.

"I'm not coming down with that thing there," Paddy shouted, pointing to the dog. "He'll fuckin' eat me. Get rid or ah'm staying up here." Hopefully this diversion would give his mate some breathing space and give him time to rescue his trousers to maybe preserve some of his dignity.

"Oh, we've got a right one here," said the cop holding the dog. "Listen, laddie, if I let this bugger go he'll be up that tree quicker than a rat up a drainpipe. So you just get yourself down here and no more nonsense."

"Gerrroooonimo!" shouted Paddy as he launched himself out of the huge chestnut tree to the amusement of the two cops, who thought they'd seen it all.

A less stalwart fifteen-year-old would have been terrified at being detained and questioned overnight and, despite the fact that he was still a minor who should be accompanied by an adult, Paddy spent the night in Maryhill cop shop. No way would he admit to anything and he appeared to be completely unfazed by the whole episode.

Pete McClelland and Paddy had joined forces when Pete had started work in his uncle's coalyard. They'd hit it off right away when Paddy had come to his rescue while Pete was taking a beating from a local mob. Almost every street in Glasgow was ruled by gangs. Crossing from one street to another was fraught with danger. Young Pete had no alternative but to pass through enemy lines on his way to and from work and on the second day he was captured.

Had it not been for Paddy's intervention it would have been doubtful that the lad would have come out alive.

Pete McClelland was a cunning, devious character and it was he, who first came up with the means to supplement their income. The boys had carried out a dozen or so break-ins over the course of the past six months and it looked like Sergeant Brown and PC Kelly had just struck gold.

For months the series of burglaries had stumped local detectives. Whoever was carrying out the crimes was extremely well informed, knew exactly when to hit and how to gain entry. They had even gone as far as robbing the provost's gaff which was taken as a personal insult.

The cops had pulled in all of the usual suspects for questioning, but got no results. Discovering the whole constabulary had been duped by a couple of delivery boys was a real redder and the twosome were in for a rough time. There would be no mercy shown by the embarrassed officials.

The lads had an ingenious modus operandi. No-one ever paid much attention to the coalman; customers were more intent on counting the bags to make sure they weren't being diddled. It was, therefore, highly unlikely a customer would recognise their coal men, especially with clean faces. The two lads simply took note of when the inhabitants were out, or away, and paid them an extra visit.

If the Coyle lad hadn't lost his keks the twosome

would have been on their toes with this haul also and god knows when they would have been apprehended. The police knew there were definitely two of them and as Paddy was caught empty-handed, someone had escaped. It hadn't taken a Philadelphia lawyer to work out who his side-kick was. His best mate and co-delivery boy was caught red-handed with the stolen goods under his bed!

Paddy couldn't believe it. How fucking stupid had Pete been?

"Fuck, I'm surprised they didn't find you hiding under there as well," he sneered at the other lad. "Hiding from the bogey man?"

Pete had never been the brains of the operation, but even so, Paddy argued, common sense should have told him to keep everything away from his home.

"Why didn't you stash them?" prodded Paddy. "Why didn't you go straight to the graveyard? If they hadn't caught you with the gear they couldn't prove anything."

"Shut up," sulked Pete. "I just panicked. They were at my house so fast somebody must have grassed me up, I hope it wasn't you."

"Don't talk fucking rubbish. I'm your best mate. Why would I grass you up? I had nothing on me," said Paddy. "All they could do me for was climbing a fucking tree or flashing my todger at passersby. But they go to visit my best pal and what do they find?"

"I said shut up."

"Tell me, what did they find? A fucking dolly mixture tin with £300 and over a grand's worth of jewellery from the house that's just been done, with my fingerprints over everything? Bang goes the tree theory. It's not exactly the workings of a pair of international jewel thieves, now is it?"

They were sentenced to eighteen months in Polmont Young Offenders. From day one it was obvious Pete was not going to cope with borstal life. It looked like the big lad was going to have to fight not only his own battles but his mate's too.

Fortunately they had been assigned to the same hall and neighbouring cells which made their introduction to prison life almost bearable, but the pecking order had to be established. Within the first forty-eight hours the twosome had to fight their way through the hall and as far as Paddy was concerned, enough was enough.

The only way he could see to survive was to attack before being attacked. So on the fourth day of their detention Paddy, armed with a sock and a billiard ball, went looking for the main man.

Robbie Carlyle was a complete nutter, a vicious psychotic fucking mental case who feared no-one. He had been top dog for the past year, terrorising even the bravest of inmates, and he ruled the hall, with the aid of his team of enforcers. Nothing happened without his say so; from drugs to booze, even visits were at his whim.

But Carlyle had never in his depraved young life come across the likes of Paddy Coyle. He was a real hard case, a man, not a boy, and one who was totally fearless. By the time Carlyle was discharged from the prison hospital Paddy was well established.

Prison life wasn't too bad; it was more tedious than anything. Having adopted the mantle vacated by Carlyle, Paddy had few complaints. Compared to his usual living conditions, this was positively five stars with all mod cons.

There was a fully equipped gym, a library, three square meals a day and he didn't have to shift thirty tons of coal to earn it. Paddy intended to make good use of his time away from home; he would come out a more educated man.

He was a big strong lad due to his coal-carrying days which stood him in good stead. Within a few weeks there was no-one fitter or more intimidating than him.

The borstal was close enough for his mother and the twins to visit frequently and occasionally they brought his new sister, baby Marie. She was just the most beautiful child. Her brothers adored and spoiled her, especially the eldest. Although things for the family were hard, thanks to Paddy's foresight there was enough in the 'stash' to keep them going, hopefully till he got out.

His main problem was Pete. He was his mate and he couldn't just leave him hanging out to dry. But the idiot had made enemy after enemy trading on Paddy's name. In fact, there were more inmates who held a grudge against him than not. He just didn't know when to leave it.

There was always someone not giving him respect. Or he was not getting what he thought was his due, but worse, he was getting a reputation for picking his victims. It seemed he was preying on the more vulnerable youngsters and this was a definite no no. No matter how often Paddy tried to keep things together, he would have to give some lad a dig. More often than not, one who often didn't deserve it, but who, poor sod, just happened to be on the receiving end of Pete McClelland's spite.

For the most part the two lads kept their noses clean and, having served almost half their sentence, were up for release. There was no reason why they shouldn't be home the following week. They had passed the panel and it was now a waiting game.

Thanks to Pete and his need to always settle scores, on the eve of their release a few of his enemies decided it was payback time and that he was due a little 'leaving present'. They misguidedly reckoned that Paddy wouldn't jeopardise his release. They hadn't bargained on Paddy's loyalty.

"Paddy, quick, your mate's in trouble," shouted one of the inmates, "The rec room. Quick."

Faced with four wannabes, Paddy strolled into the rec room taking in the scene. Pete had certainly taken second prize in the contest, much to Paddy's anger.

"Well well, who fancies their chances before I take my leave?" he asked the group. "No-one? Okay, well one for all as they say," and Paddy steamed in amongst them.

In front of the governor the following morning there was no disguising what had happened and certainly no-one would believe that four inmates had fallen down stairs, all at the same time.

Paddy was there for the duration, and Pete - well he was enjoying a celebration drink in the Guardsman pub with his da and his mates. Not a thought for Paddy Coyle or his family.

Lizzie and the twins were furious and refused to visit for weeks unable to cope with Paddy's stupidity, especially over Pete.

"How could you let that snivelling bastard involve you again?"

"Do you think for one minute he'd do the same for you?"

"C'mon, Ma, he's not a fighter," replied Paddy.

"He doesn't have to be, ya bloody eejit. He's got you, his pet boxer."

During the months he had left to serve he had only one visit from Pete and one postcard, from Benidorm. Still, Paddy made excuses for him but they were getting thin on the ground.

Nearing the end of his term he had an unexpected visit from the twins. The lads came as often as they could but due to the visiting conditions, seldom together or without their mother in tow. He could tell they were extremely agitated but trying hard to keep it together for his sake. Something major was up and things had to be desperate for them to visit this close to his release.

All the while Paddy had been away, the twins had carefully looked after his 'stash'. Each month they took just enough to pawn or sell to keep the family with a roof over their heads and food on the table.

For all the time Paddy had been away, this had

worked perfectly. Michael and Sean, although a pair of buggers, were responsible for their family's survival and took their responsibilities seriously. But when they had gone to the graveyard a couple of months previously, to collect what little was left, it had gone.

The twins and Lizzie had struggled on as best they could, keeping this news from Paddy, but the family were in dire straits. The young lads didn't know what to do. They had promised their ma and Paddy, when he was first incarcerated, that they wouldn't go on 'the rob' but things were getting desperate.

Their mother could barely cope with the present circumstances but certainly wouldn't if another of her family was put away. But what else could they do? They were all so close to the finishing line, having endured all those months, surely they weren't going to fail now?

"Go and see Pete," ordered Paddy. "Get him to lend you enough to last this month."

"No good," said Michael. "He was the first port of call but says he's got nought, mind you he's just come back from two weeks in Spain, the jammy bastard."

"I know, I got a postcard," Paddy answered.

"Paddy, who knew about the stash?" asked Sean.

"Us three and Pete."

"What does that tell you? It wouldn't take fucking Mystic Meg to know where the loot went then."

"Aye, fucking Spain," said his younger brother.

"Look, he's my best mate and he knows what that money was for, somebody must have seen you."

"No way," chimed both boys.

"No way, we were never followed. We took a different route every time. What do you think we are - a couple of Muppets?" cried Michael.

"Funny nothing happened while he was inside, but all of a sudden he can afford holidays in fucking sunny Spain."

"Aye, he doesn't have to bring a donkey home, he's got a pet one right here."

"Now we've got Ma threatening to go to Mickey Kelly for a loan."

"Not that fucking shark, we'll still be paying the interest off with my pension," shouted Paddy, drawing the attention of two of the screws.

"Everything okay lads?" asked one.

"Aye fine, ma mother's just won the lottery and we're wondering if we can buy him out early. Any chance?"

"Any more smart remarks and you'll be keeping your brother company."

"Oh, yer letting him out then?" smirked Sean.

"Can it you two. What about Dad's bits and pieces? Is there anything worth selling?"

All gone, said the twins.

Visiting time was over and Paddy promised his brothers he would sort something out and phone them later that night.

He needed to get hold of Pete. It was payback time.

Revenge

Completely ignoring the speed restrictions, and not giving a toss whether they drew attention to themselves or not, the convoy of vehicles sped through Glasgow city centre. Paddy, grasping the shred of blood-stained netting, was stony faced and silent. The big man didn't trust himself to speak. His brothers, too, were silent, dreading what the significance of the veil meant. *Christ alone help us if they've hurt Erin.*

There were few rules amongst the gangs and certainly not much of a code of ethics but women and children were never to be involved. It would seem the McClellands had crossed that line.

Turning into the street, the way was blocked with police cars, ambulances, paramedics and a bloody helicopter flying overhead; it was like a scene from a Hollywood blockbuster. But this was real life. Racing from his vehicle, Paddy dashed back and forth looking for his wife and kid, almost passing out with dread when he saw his girl drenched in blood.

"She's okay, Paddy she's okay," screamed Bridget. "It's not her blood. She's okay."

"What happened, who did this?" roared Paddy as if he didn't know. Grabbing his girl and holding her tight to his chest, "Daddy's here darling. Daddy's here, speak to me, are you okay, are you hurt? Christ, look at the fucking state of her, Bridget. What in God's name happened, who's hurt?"

Erin didn't utter a word.

"Oh Paddy," Bridget sobbed, "she was having a wonderful day. She wanted to help Jamesie out in the van. I should have said no, I shouldn't have let her, but I never thought. Oh! Paddy if we'd lost her. Oh my god," Bridget was inconsolable.

Michael came running to his brothers' side. "Marie's in a bad way Paddy, she tried to stop one of the cunts and caught it full blast, it's not looking good. She's on her way to the Royal. I'm going there now. Jamesie wasn't so lucky, poor fucker, one of the boys better go see his old ma."

"Anyone else?" asked the big man.

"Aye, Father Jack, he's been taken to the Southern General, I think it was his heart. We were set up Paddy, the bastards set us up."

Like a general on a battlefield Paddy Coyle took charge. The green was stripped of the tables and makeshift bar, much to the disgust of a couple of old jakies who were completely oblivious to the carnage. Paddy descended on them like the wrath of God. Picking one up and throwing him across the green, he turned his attention to the other, who, not having the sense to shut up and fuck off, was protesting loudly at the treatment of his buddy while necking his pal's drink.

Paddy Coyle was one of the most feared men in Glasgow. In a city full of hard men there were few who would ever cross him and right now the need to vent his anger was uncontrollable. He had half-killed the drunk in full view of at least two dozen police officers, but none would have dared approach him.

"The fucking nerve of them," roared Paddy, banging his fist on the table with such force he almost cleaved it in two. "Coming to my fucking turf, shooting at my fucking family. They're dead, every last fucking one of them dead."

Paddy was beyond reason and those sitting round the table knew he had good reason to be. McClelland's actions today were mugging them off, showing the rest of Glasgow that the McClellands were no marks and that Paddy couldn't defend his own people.

A council of war had been summoned and Paddy's clan were assembled in Lizzie's kitchen. The news from the hospital on Marie was not too promising and their mother would not leave her daughter's bedside. One side of Marie's body had taken the full force of the shot.

Bridget had taken Erin home and Paddy sent Teresa to see how Father Jack was faring. Shame it hadn't been the other old cunt. The two old guys he'd joked with earlier that day had flesh wounds and were being kept in hospital overnight for observation. Teresa volunteered to check on them also.

"I want that bastard McClelland taken out once and for all. He's gone too fucking far this time and he's making a cunt of us. I want him finished. Davey, Johnny Boy and two of your best, put the vans out of action. Torch the place. He's going to know we'll come after him so we won't have the element of surprise, just plain brute force. Go in all guns blazing. I want fuck-all left."

"Next, his house, I'll go with Sean, I want to see it burn."

Later that night, the smoke could be seen all across the Glasgow skyline.

By the end of the week, word on the street was Pete McClelland had gone. No-one knew for sure where, but with his businesses finished and his home torched, the pubs, clubs and saunas that had been under his protection were either reduced to ashes or now part of the Coyle Corporation. Only a very few of his men were still on his payroll and they were conspicuous by their absence. There was nothing left in Glasgow for him. Like thieves in the night, the McClelland family disappeared.

What Pete had worked for all these years was gone, there was nothing left. Coyle had moved in and destroyed him. Why? There had been no love lost between them for years not since just after Paddy's discharge from borstal. Yeah he supposed he could have done a bit more to help, but what was he, a fucking babysitter? The truth was he'd got in tow with some old boiler and was in shagging heaven. At seventeen with his hormones racing, fuck-all else in the world existed.

Aye, he'd felt a bit guilty that Paddy's family had it fucking rough, but so did everybody in those days. His mate had been out only a few weeks and walked straight into a job with Mickey Kelly. So what the fuck was his beef? If it hadn't been for him, Pete reasoned, the big man would still be carrying bags of coal; in reality he'd done him a favour.

Taking McClelland out had been too easy. No resistance, no fight, no retaliation. It was as if McClelland had just lain down and accepted his fate, either that or he didn't know it was coming. No way, the cunt must have known, no-one in their right minds would believe Paddy Coyle would not seek revenge, especially when it concerned family.

Paddy

It had not been the best of home-comings, within an hour of his return the family had had a visit from two of Mickey Kelly's collectors demanding payment.

"A hundred quid by five o'clock or the kid gets it."

"You've been watching too many gangster films," laughed Paddy.

"Five o'clock," the biggest of the two replied.

"Fuck off man, I'm just out. I've not had time to get my shit together. No can do, tell your boss he'll get his money, I just need a bit of time."

"Four o'clock. We'll be back at four," the two men banged the door behind them.

"Fuck's sake, Ma, how much do you owe the cunts?" demanded Paddy.

"Don't blame me," his mother cried. "It was your bloody pal that got us into this mess. I'll bet he was waiting at the gate this morning with a fist full of tenners? No, I didn't think so."

"Never mind him, he'll keep," Paddy was still convinced that Pete would come good.

"Where the fuck am I going to get that kind of dosh by four o'clock?"

"Oh, Paddy, I'm sorry. Honestly if I had had a choice. I owe everybody, all the neighbours, most of the shops you name it, I owe them. It's been hellish."

"You still haven't said how much we owe."

"Honest, son, I don't know, but I can tell you, delivering milk isn't going to pay our debts off."

At four o'clock exactly came a knock at the door.

Paddy had been home for almost a week before he caught up with his best mate. Strolling along Sauchiehall Street with the latest bird on his arm, a sheepish McClelland came face to face with his old pal.

"Hey mate, how're you doing? He said slapping Paddy on the back. "I was just on my way to see you," blustered Pete. "This is Fiona. Say hello to Paddy, Fiona. Sorry I've not been about but you know how it is, busy, busy. I was giving you time to settle in," crawled an anxious McClelland.

Survival was the name of the game and without Paddy at his back the snivelling coward knew he had no chance. He had meant to call in and see Paddy but the time just disappeared, and with his latest crush, well! McClelland had joined forces with a gang from his own neck of the woods which pretty much left Paddy out in the cold.

Knowing full well he had let his old mate down, Pete babbled on in the hope he could talk Paddy round.

"C'mon, let me buy you a drink, pal, and we'll catch up."

Paddy didn't utter a word.

"Honest, it's great to see you Paddy, I've really missed you, but what the fuck's happened? You look like you've been in the wars; who have you been upsetting?" Shit! McClelland could have bitten his tongue seeing the expression on Paddy's face.

"But," he blundered on, hope fading. "How are you fixed, big man? Here, that should see you alright," as he offered him a bundle of notes.

Fiona seemed none too pleased at the sudden generosity of her companion. She'd had her eye on a smart jacket in Lewis's window and was hoping to persuade Pete she just had to have it.

"Excuse me, darling," as Paddy turned away from the girl and with one punch knocked his ex-best mate clean out. He walked off, leaving a bewildered Fiona busy gathering up scattered ten pound notes and an unconscious McClelland to fend for themselves on the busy Glasgow street.

Canon Francis O'Farrell

Canon O'Farrell watched in wry amusement as the Coyle clan went haring off to the other side of the city, leaving a furious wife and mother. Disrupting the enjoyment of not only the family, but that of neighbours and all the scoundrels and misfits on Coyle's payroll, on what the priest knew to be a wild goose chase.

How did he know? In exactly the same way that he knew the blacked out vehicle that had just pulled up behind the ice cream van would arrive when it did. That it would contain three gunmen, whose orders were to render the van and its contents out of commission and to make sure that he, Canon Francis O'Farrell was well out of range. How did he know there would be no-one left at the celebration able to stop this happening, or that Paddy Coyle wouldn't just send his lieutenants to deal with the problems with the Police? He just knew!

What didn't amuse him was the feckin' stupidity

of his understudy, Father Jack, getting so bloody het up about the situation. Not only did the eejit suddenly become a 'have-a-go-hero', but even more stupidly, he'd gone and had a feckin' heart attack in the midst of all the chaos.

Christ, the stupid fecker could be out of commission for weeks, months even, and that would certainly throw a bloody great spanner in the works where he was concerned.

Father Francis O'Farrell had been seconded to the city of Glasgow not long after he had left the seminary. His first impression of Craigloch was that of a dank and dreary outpost. For a lad brought up in the magnificent landscape of Galway, with its wild terrain and rugged countryside, it would definitely be a trial. But he was there for a purpose and it wasn't just to serve God.

For generations the O'Farrells had been staunch anti-royalists, and all but he were active soldiers in the Irish Republican Army.

His two elder brothers were on the Council and the youngest was languishing in Mount Joy Jail, where he would stay incarcerated for the next fifteen years. The powers that be had decreed that St. Jude's in Craigloch was the ideal safe haven for those loyal Irish men on the move and Father Francis O'Farrell was the very man to accommodate them.

Just off the boat, the young priest was thrown right in at the deep end and it was then his hatred for the Coyle family began.

His superior, Canon Thomas, was a decrepit old

soul who had been resident in Craigloch for over fifty years. He was once a vibrant, passionate minister who worked tirelessly for his parishioners, but by the time Father Francis arrived the old man spent most of his time asleep in the confessional, completely oblivious to the comings and goings of his staff or his fellow countrymen.

To further ensure confidentiality and allay any suspicions concerning the goings on, a widow woman from the same village as Father Francis was co-opted to look after the domestic arrangements. Mrs Gavin had lost two of her sons to the Cause and hated Protestants and the English in equal measures. For years this arrangement worked perfectly. For escapees, and for those who had to move on, St Jude's was the perfect solution.

The parish had for many years been a training ground for young men intent on entering the priesthood, so to slip a few cuckoos into the nest didn't stir up too much curiosity. From time to time a parishioner would question the validity of a 'guest' but few would chance Father O'Farrell's lethal tongue at their curiosity.

These guests had been of great use to the Father over the years just as they had today.

He would never jeopardise the operation or draw attention to his house guests, but he had kept more than one pot boiling over the years. He would stir up grievances with occasional forays into forbidden territories. He kept the Glasgow Criminal Fraternity on its toes. A quiet word here, an innocent nudge there, had blameless individuals at the mercy of one gang boss or another. No-one ever suspecting for a moment the deviousness of the good father.

The old feud between the Coyles and the McClellands would have died out years ago but for the machinations of Paddy Coyle's oldest enemy. The list of incidents was endless and there existed a virtual tit-for-tat culture between the two families and a deep hatred of one another. The war between them had, thanks to the priest, taken on momentous proportions and today was the proverbial last straw. For the McClellands, unbeknown to them, it was the end of their reign in Glasgow and the Coyles would follow soon. Unfortunately, thanks to Father Jack's unexpected collapse, the Coyles had received a stay of execution.

Paddy

True to their promise, at four o'clock prompt, the front door crashed in. Paddy had already sent his mother and baby Marie through to Teresa next door. The twins, refusing to leave their brother, were each armed with the ubiquitous baseball bat. The three Coyle brothers for the first time stood together waiting, but not for long. As soon as the two goons showed their faces, Paddy flew into action; he was a one man wrecking machine. This lad could fight, really, really fight. Swinging the bat with all his strength, smashing bone, cracking skulls, raining down blows, this was no ordinary skirmish. His opponents couldn't get near him.

His brothers stood back in amazement; they had never witnessed anything like it. Sure, they knew Paddy could handle himself, but this? This was phenomenal; brutal, vicious, terrifying and almost primeval. Paddy beat the two debt collectors to a pulp. The fight itself probably lasted no more than five minutes and their mother's kitchen looked like the inside of an abattoir. Fuck, she'd go mental, thought Paddy, there was blood everywhere. But little or none belonged to a Coyle.

The neighbours were well aware of what was happening at number 28 but none felt inclined to get involved. Young lads or no young lads, nobody was likely to come to their aid. Lizzie was sick to her stomach at the prospect of her sons being hurt, especially when she knew it was she who had got them into this mess and from the noises emanating from her house, there were murders going on. Unable to stand by any longer, she dumped baby Marie on Teresa, and armed with a fireside poker (the Glasgow woman's weapon of choice), stormed into her house. She was met by two great lumps of bleeding and battered manhood, but her sons were intact.

"Look at the state of my feckin' kitchen," she bellowed at the threesome. "Get this bloody lot cleared up before I bring the baby back, and as for you two, fuck off back to where you came," as she stormed back next door, secretly glowing with pride at her boys. Thank God Paddy was home.

Kicking their would-be assailants out into the street, the brothers, whooping with glee, chased them off. Paddy knew it would be a short-lived celebration. It was only a matter of time before Kelly's reinforcements would arrive and they would definitely come mob handed. The lads wouldn't be let off so easily next time and their actions had probably incurred even more debt. He had to sort it and it had to be with Mickey Kelly himself and on Kelly's territory. Paddy knew there was every chance he might not get out alive.

Ensconced in the back room of his favourite pub the Tower Inn, a dingy back street watering hole favoured by most of the 'Faces' from the surrounding area, Mickey Kelly had just been apprised of the fate of his two main collectors.

"What the fuck do you mean the boys took a hammering?" Mickey Kelly shouted at the bearer of the news.

"Don't shoot the fucking messenger," Lisa the barmaid shouted back. "And it was a couple of schoolboys who did it," she smirked.

"Fuck off, ya cheeky fat bastard," he growled at Lisa. "No way. Is somebody having a laugh? You couldn't put that pair down with a steamroller, never mind the whole of sixth year at St. Jude's. A couple of schoolboys? I don't fucking think so."

"Well, where are they then?" Lisa retaliated. "I don't see them, do you? Maybe they're collecting the dinner money off the first years," she laughed uproariously.

She was the only one who could get away with speaking to Mickey like this. Rumour had it that they had been married at one time, but neither would confirm or deny the fact. No-one else in the room dared laugh or even speak for that matter. Mickey Kelly was one mean bastard and reputed to be the biggest loan shark in the city. Nobody got away with a farthing from Mickey, his motto being 'don't pay, don't walk' and there were many, many crutches, courtesy of Mickey Kelly.

Whatever the story was, Kelly had to get it sorted. In his business it was all about face. If he let these fuckers take the piss, he might as well shut up shop and there was no way he was doing that.

"Hey, Mickey, a visitor," shouted Lisa from the other bar. "It's the milk monitor from St. Jude's to see you."

"Go on through, son. Don't let him know you're scared and you'll be fine. Stand up to the gobshite. Remember, you won, not 'Dumb and Dumber'."

As Paddy entered the room he took a hefty blow to the back of his head and without flinching he turned to face the loan shark.

"I'll give you that one Mr Kelly, but I'll tell you what I told your goons as they were leaving, if you ever lay a finger on me or mine again, I will retaliate."

"Fuck, I'm shaking in my boots. You'll retaliate, will you? What makes you think you'll leave this room alive, boy?"

There were at least ten other occupants in the lounge bar, all of whom looked like they could have a dash. Paddy thought he might have bitten off more than he could chew.

"I know I'm safe because my family owes you money and there is no way, whatever I've done, that you are going to jeopardise being paid, not if you're the astute business man I believe you are. So as long as my family owes you, I'm safe."

No-one spoke, in fact few were breathing, the tension was unbearable, but he kept his nerve.

"You cheeky young cunt," Mickey roared with laughter. "You've got some neck on you but you're right, there's no fucking way I'm putting you out of commission till the debt is paid in full."

"I know sir; I also know you're two men down," and turning to the assembled crew. "Sorry guys but if they were the best, fuck knows how you have survived this long."

"What you saying boy?" asked Kelly. "You saying you could take any of my guys?"

"Yes sir," said Paddy promptly. "I take it you won't have to check my references; you already know what my credentials are, so when do I start?"

Seldom was Mickey Kelly ever dumbstruck, but this time he was. He'd never met the like. An eighteen year old laddie challenging his crew and telling him that he'd take a job, what a fucking brahma; he'd tell this story for years. The kid was in, no doubt about it. Either that or one of his opposition would snap him up. Mickey would rather Big Paddy Coyle was with him not against him and there were few he'd admit that little gem to.

The Twins

The Coyle twins were a pair of little feckers, according to their mother, their brother, their teachers, in fact almost, without exception, the rest of their known world. From the moment they could walk they were up and away, there was no holding them back. If there was mischief afoot you could bet your last halfpenny that those two little buggers had planned, executed, or benefited from whatever act had caused agg to someone. They were, however, the most adorable little buggers in the street and liked by one and all, despite the mayhem they caused on a daily basis.

Always laughing, always happy and whatever they were up to, it was usually sheer devilment. Between them they had everyone run ragged. You never saw one but the other would be right behind.

Everyone just called them "The Twins". Very seldom were they referred to by their first names, Sean and Michael. In fact, few of their neighbours actually knew their first names, it was always 'Coyle Twin' to either.

They were typical little city boys, stocky, red-headed, cocky little monsters with quite a swagger and absolutely identical. Only their mother and their older brother Patrick could tell them apart, and even they had difficulty at times. To everyone else connected with them, it was 'a Twin' who 'dunnit'. In school, to assist the teachers, they were made to wear coloured ribbons on their jumpers. Yellow for Sean and red for Michael, but they swapped them with such regularity that the exercise was soon abandoned.

By the age of five they knew the surrounding streets like the backs of their hands, every nook and cranny and they scavenged them like a pair of professional Tallymen. They never returned home without some prize or another, much to the gratitude of their beleaguered mother. They 'rescued' anything from old bicycle frames to live chickens. Everything had a value to the lads and every penny helped their needy family. Recycling came as naturally as breathing to the twins.

Their mother, Patrick and baby Marie were the total sum of their world and the man called Da was seldom seen by the boys. A fleeting figure who appeared from nowhere, unexpectedly, with treats and presents galore. A man who threw everyone's lives into chaos. Their ma was a completely different person when he was around. Not the strict disciplinarian who made them eat all their dinner, made them go to bed early, who kept them safe and who spent her days looking out for them. No, this woman was different, she even smelled different. No longer 'the boss', she deferred to him; what he said went. She spent less time with her boys and more time on tarting herself up. Then, just when they were used to him being in their lives, off he'd go, disappearing as unexpectedly as he had arrived, leaving a trail of debts and distress. It would take their ma weeks to get back to normal.

Other boys had fathers who played footie with them, or took them on fishing trips to nearby Loch Lomond or to the banks of the well-polluted River Clyde. Not theirs, he was never sober enough, or around long enough. But so what? They had Paddy and the other boys could keep their fishing trips and footie, Paddy was their hero. No-one in the whole of the East End could fight like their brother. Nobody ever picked on them when they found out they were Paddy Coyle's brothers. They reckoned their Paddy was going to be heavyweight champion of the world.

The family would live in a mansion on Dumbarton Road. They would eat ice cream every day, have brand new Chopper bikes and never have to go to school. That bastard Father O'Farrell would be sacked and sent back to Ireland. Ma would have a new coat for every day of the week and baby Marie would be dressed like a Princess.

Despite their dad's interference and interruption in the boys' daily lives, they still trailed and scavenged their territory like fully fledged second-hand dealers, bringing in three or four pounds a week, an amount not to be sniffed at. Unfortunately, not enough for the mansion, and the nearest to Dumbarton Road any of the family were likely to reach was the tree their Paddy had fallen out of when he got nicked for being on the rob.

How life changed without Paddy. For a start, the twins had to fight their own battles, and every day seemed to be a round of skirmishes. They had not quite inherited their brother's fighting acumen, but they could certainly hold their own in the playground. But it was a different story in the classroom. The boys were the relentless targets of both Father O'Farrell and Sister Mary-Claire.

Eighteen months is a long time when things are bad and things had gotten decidedly so in the last few months of Paddy's sojourn. Their brother had been on to a good thing with McClelland and over the course of the year had amassed a tidy sum in ill-gotten gains. Unlike McClelland, who spent as he earned, Paddy had made a promise to himself, come hell or high water, none of them would ever go short again. Somehow, he would earn big money; he would have a swanky car and live in a big house out in the country. His dream, unlike the twins, had nothing to do with boxing, but it might well have to do with fighting, Paddy's only real talent. Young as he was, he knew he had to have stake money, so almost everything he earned from being on the rob had been squirreled away, almost untouched.

It was this foresight that had kept the Coyle family afloat. The twins had managed the finances with the expertise of a city accountant till some bastard stitched them up, and they were damned sure they knew who it was.

First Job

For all his bravado, Paddy Coyle was absolutely terrified approaching the imposing house belonging to Mad Billy Mitchell. It was 6.30 on a Sunday morning and Mad Billy's Mercedes was abandoned in the drive. A couple of Dobermans were snoring gently just in front of it; out for the count thanks to a couple of sirloin steaks liberally doused with Lizzie's sleeping pills. Paddy reckoned he'd at least an hour before the brutes came to.

He had spent most of yesterday doing a reccie on the property and decided the easiest route in was straight through one of the ground floor windows. There were several marble statues dotted around the beautifully landscaped gardens and one of these would certainly do the trick. Out of curiosity, as you never know your luck, he turned the huge handle on the front door. To his surprise the door swung open. Paddy couldn't believe his luck. Presumably the occupants reckoned they were safe with the dogs wandering the grounds.

Wrong! Holding back a few minutes, he listened for the beep of an alarm . . . nothing. Why have all these elaborate systems and then not bother to turn the fuckers on, he mused?

Quietly making his way upstairs, Paddy walked slap bang into a small, blonde middle-aged woman, stark naked holding a glass of water and a white fluffy animal. She screamed and dropped the water; he screamed even louder and smacked her on the chin. His signature punch! She was out cold.

Oh fuck! Oh Mother of God, help me. He was almost dancing with fright; he had to get rid of her and shut that fucking animal up or it would waken the dead. Slinging her over his shoulder he chucked the unconscious woman, who he presumed was Mad Billy's wife, onto a bed in an empty bedroom. Fuck, she should be covered up, she certainly wasn't a natural blonde, not from what he'd seen. Shit, that image would put him off sex for months. Picking up the yapping bundle, he tossed it into the room and closed the door.

Mad Billy had a number of saunas around the city and from the look of the house and gardens, they obviously paid well. The interior was even more impressive than the outside. So why was the stupid bastard holding out on a measly five thousand to Mickey Kelly? It didn't make sense and from what Paddy had heard, Mickey was getting beyond just collecting the money on this one. The man was taking the piss. Whatever the reason, Paddy was there to recover the debt and if there was a bit extra, then that would be a bonus.

The man wasn't called Mad Billy for nothing. He had a reputation going back years and there were few men who would go against him, so this was Paddy's deal breaker. He had to recoup the loan, a real baptism of fire. His only chance of success was the element of surprise.

On a face to face, Paddy stood no chance. Mitchell was always tooled up.

Mitchell had returned home just after four this morning, surely there was no chance he would be up and about a mere two hours later? The likelihood of his being awake was slim but Paddy was taking no chances, he had to get this over quick.

Snoring like an express train, lying face down on the king size bed was his quarry. Paddy had him bound, gagged and gaffer-taped to the only chair in the bedroom before Mitchell knew what had hit him. Drenching him with water, Mad Billy came to cursing and swearing as best he could. Whoever the fuck had done this to him had better make a good job, because when he got free, and he would, he would fucking murder the bastard.

"Good morning Mr Mitchell, I'm so sorry if I've disturbed your sleep, but I'm here on Mr Kelly's orders, a little matter of five thousand owing to the gentleman." Paddy was so polite and had adopted a real Kelvinside accent. It was comical, although the other party didn't seem to find the situation the least bit amusing.

"This matter can be settled quickly and painlessly or not; the decision, Mr Mitchell, is entirely yours.

But I should tell you that I will be leaving with either the five thousand, your testicles, or both."

Mad Billy Mitchell was more than mad; he was fucking livid. A fucking boy scout standing in his gaff demanding a piddling five thousand quid. What the fuck was Glasgow coming to? Okay he should have coughed up to Mitchell a couple of weeks back. But the miserable cunt knew he was good for the money. In fact, why he'd borrowed the wedge in the first place completely escaped him. He must have been out of his face to even speak to the cunt, never mind tap him for some dosh. Heaven help Kelly and this two bit cowboy when he got out of this mess.

The kid was prattling on about fuck knows what, Billy had only cottoned on to a couple of sentences about testicles and safes. His head was thumping and he was still half coked from last night, actually it was from this morning. But guys like Mad Billy didn't stay on top without having a few tricks up their sleeves; one of Billy's party pieces was being able to get out of almost any bondage, to the dismay of many would be assailants. Paddy wouldn't be the first to be astounded at Billy's Houdini act.

Not too discreetly, the captive was busily trying to free himself, all the time screaming and cursing at the top of his voice and promising to fuckin' maul this upstart. Twisting and turning to no avail, the mad man had to give up; he was well and truly immobilized. Paddy had long ago heard of Mitchell's famous escapades and made bloody sure he wouldn't be springing any surprises on him.

Over an hour of systematic beatings and no result, Paddy withdrew to rethink his strategy. This was certainly not what he'd signed up for. Mad Billy Mitchell looked like something out of a fucking horror movie. His face, unrecognisable and almost twice its normal size, a suppurating mess of raw flesh, his left eye looked damaged beyond repair. Still the captive was taunting and cursing the amateur collector. Billy Mitchell knew that Paddy was new to the game.

Paddy had presumed that it was a case of in, demand money with some menacing and then out. Not fucking hammering somebody half to death and they still wouldn't give out. Paddy was no nearer to getting the safe combination than he was when he arrived. He had no idea what to do next and Mitchell knew that.

Moaning from the next room alerted him to the other occupant of the house. Carrying the screaming clawing banshee into the room Paddy was sure this would sort Mitchell out. If he wouldn't give in, then the wife would get hurt. Mitchell, despite the state of him, roared with laughter.

"Go on son, do your worst. I fucking hate the fat old bastard. Hey, in fact, do her and I'll double what Kelly was paying. Look at it, would you save that? No fucking chance. You'll save me fucking thousands in the divorce courts."

Paddy was flummoxed, he really didn't know what to do next, the body on the bed was screeching and bellowing; he could see what Mitchell meant, she really was an ugly old fucker. But if he couldn't pull this job off he was in the shit.

The wife and her beloved husband were taking the piss big time, neither would save the other. She hated him as much as he hated her, maybe even more.

This was getting ridiculous, what the fuck was he going to do?

"If that dog doesn't stop fucking yapping, I'm gonna break its neck."

"No! No, not Poochy," wailed the wife. "Don't hurt her, whatever you want to know I'll tell you. Just don't harm my baby."

Paddy looked gormlessly at the wailing, pleading woman. Poochy? Who the fuck was Poochy? Paddy was baffled. Christ, it was the fucking mutt, "Thank you, God."

"Give me the combination now or Poochy gets it," shouted Paddy. "Now, or it's curtains," grabbing the little dog by the scruff of the neck.

He was out of the house and legging it five minutes later to his getaway vehicle, the number 42 bus to Glasgow Cross.

He arrived home just after nine, as his mother, back from mass, was cooking breakfast. Paddy was exhausted but delirious. What a result. He was on an adrenalin rush like he'd never experienced before. Christ, he was up and down like a bloody fiddler's elbow and couldn't sit still, dying to get his mother out of the way to see what he'd got away with.

"What the hell is up with you?" asked his ma. "You're like a bloody cat on a hot tin roof and look at the state of you. What the devil is that you're covered in?"

"It's nothing, Ma, for God's sake, give it a rest."

"Oh Mary, Mother of God, it's blood. Oh, my God, what have you been up to? For heaven's sake, boy you're just out. Don't go getting yourself back into trouble, son. I couldn't go through that again."

"I'm not going anywhere. Let me get changed and we'll talk," he assured his mother.

Ten minutes later, freshly dressed, shaved and devouring the heaped plate of food put down in front of him, the morning's activities had certainly not diminished his appetite.

"Right, my lad, what exactly have you been up to and whose blood was that?"

"Jesus, Ma, it's like the Spanish Inquisition. I was earning, that's all you need to know," He threw a couple of twenty pound notes across the table at her. "Will that ease your conscience any?"

"How dare you, how bloody dare you?" Lizzie yelled, slapping him hard round the ear. "Don't you ever speak to me like that or treat me like one of your stupid mates. Do you think forty quid is going to make me condone your beating someone up for money? Would you come and beat up me and baby Marie if we got behind with Mr Big Shot Kelly? Because that nearly happened, didn't it?"

"Aye, Ma, that nearly did happen, but thank fuck for you lot, I can fight our way out of trouble."

Another clout round the ear and Paddy was up and towering over his mother.

"Don't you ever lift your hand to me again, or so help me, I'll forget you're my mother," he snarled.

There was no way Lizzie Coyle would ever back down to anyone and especially not this gormless big lump of shite she called her son.

She gave him another belt round the ear. Paddy was incensed and God knows what would have happened but for the arrival of Sean carrying baby Marie. "What's going on? You wakened the wee one, we could hear you two going at it good style," said Sean.

"Paddy, Paddy." Marie had her arms outstretched for Paddy to take her. But her beloved brother stormed past and out of the room.

"What's up, Ma?" Sean questioned her. "And don't say nothing, I've not seen him like that for a long time."

"It really is nothing, son. He just forgot who he was talking to and I gave him a sharp reminder," smiled Lizzie. By God, she'd forgot what a stubborn bugger that son of hers could be, but he'd forgot who had fought for them all these past years. Lizzie Coyle would stand up to Auld Nick himself to keep her kids safe and Patrick Joseph Coyle had just been reminded of that fact.

He had to calm himself down. Christ he'd nearly hit his mother, he could hardly believe it. He wouldn't ever harm a hair on her head and dear God; he'd never forgive himself if he had hurt her, but what an aggravating fucker she could be. Paddy knew his mother would stand by him no matter what, but he wouldn't tolerate anyone laying hands on him, not even her.

What a fucking day it had turned out. He'd half-killed a man, taken the wife and dog prisoner, legged it with more money than he'd ever seen in his entire life, almost mullered his ma, brought his breakfast up and Jesus, it was only 10 o'clock on a Sunday morning. Paddy Coyle was buzzing.

He was gobsmacked at how much he'd got away with: a good few grand's worth of jewellery and almost twenty thousand in cash − four times the five thousand pounds debt. He'd got a fucking good haul and there was no way he was handing all this lot over to Mickey Kelly. He'd certainly need to give the loan shark what he was owed, but as for the rest? Who could prove what was in the safe? It was his word against Billy's and as long as Paddy wasn't too greedy, Kelly would be satisfied.

Carrying coal or delivering milk was way behind him now, he was heading for the big time. He knew he'd been lucky this morning; he needed a partner or partners and who better than his brothers, if they were up to it?

Lizzie

Thank God her boy was home. He'd got that bugger Kelly off her back and within weeks, she'd managed to clear most of her debts with the local shopkeepers but, more importantly, with her neighbours. Oh, she knew they had all been in her situation at one time or another and she had always been the first to help out. But it was a different kettle of fish when it was she who owed. Thanks to Paddy she could hold her head up, knowing she was debt-free and the comfort of having a few extra pounds in her purse was something she'd seldom known.

The downside of her newfound wealth was Paddy's involvement with the Kelly mob. It was obvious he was working off the debt and for that she would be eternally grateful, but he was a changed boy. For a start he was no longer a boy. From the day he started working with this outfit something had gone from Paddy, mainly his youth and what innocence he had left.

The bugger had always got into scrapes, they all did, but in the past she'd never known Paddy to start a fight. He might always finish it and there were a few sorry devils who regretted throwing the first punch but it was different now, he was different. She hated that he was being paid to hurt people, mostly people like them who'd got into difficulties and she didn't like it. She wanted her boy back, but that was never going to happen; the die was cast.

"Do me a shirt, Ma, I'm going out in half an hour" said Paddy grabbing his wee mother and twirling her round the kitchen to the great amusement of his baby sister sitting on a rug by the blazing fire.

"Me, me, 'addy," she squealed, arms akimbo. "Me peese."

None of the boys could refuse Marie anything. She was such a cutie and at the tender age of two could wrap her brothers, or any man for that matter, round her sticky little fingers. A lesson she would use to her advantage for the rest of her life.

Swinging the little girl round and round, squealing at the top of her voice, their mother looked on lovingly. If it could only stay like this, Lizzie thought. She had one of her 'feelings' something was going to happen and she was seldom wrong.

The boys all laughed at their ma's predictions, never taking them seriously, but Lizzie did, and there was something coming, she could feel it in her bones.

"Take the night off, Paddy, stay at home with us. We'll get a video and some beers and . . ."

"You been on the old communion wine, Ma?"

laughed the big lad. "It's Saturday night. Why the devil would I be staying in with my old mother and a bottle of Vimto?"

"Keep me company, son, I've got one of my feelings."

"Oh, Ma, the last time you had a feeling and were all doom and gloom, old Jimmy along the way got a first division on the coupon."

"Aye, so he did, but remember, he forgot to post it. Stay in with Marie and me just this once."

"You're not doing my street cred much good. Hey the hardest man in Glasgow watching the Von Trapp family and eating popcorn. No, it doesn't quite hit the spot Ma, but thanks anyway."

Half an hour later the three brothers, all suited and booted, were out to cause mayhem on a regular Saturday night in Glasgow, leaving their mother and baby sister on their own. She hoped she was wrong.

Rise to Fame

Despite their ma's request for them to stay home, the three lads hit the town running that Saturday night. First port of call was the Gunners, a favourite pub of the Kelly firm. A couple of drinks then they intended going on to the infamous Barrowlands dance hall.

None of the brothers were big drinkers, thanks to their da. His example had been enough. The bar was packed to the rafters but you could cut the atmosphere with a knife. There was a palpable tension in the air, something was about to go down.

Paddy walked up to the bar and ordered their drinks just as a shot rang out and the place erupted. Twenty or so interlopers from the north side of the city had ventured into foreign territory, led by his old mucker Pete McClelland, and it looked like they meant business.

What the fuck was McClelland doing on his turf? thought Paddy as he waded into the melee, scattering bodies right and left. Making for his ex-mate, he was caught by a blow on the side of his temple which floored him. Just enough time for McClelland to fire one more shot.

Tables, chairs and mirrors were smashed in the affray and there were casualties on both sides, but thanks to Paddy most of his mob escaped serious injury, all except two. Rushing to his brother he saw the damage. Some bastard with a Stanley knife had sliced Sean's face. From eye to chin, his face was wide open. Eighteen stitches later, no-one would ever have any trouble telling the twins apart again.

It was almost an hour later that Mickey Kelly was found slumped behind the heavy blackout curtains. The infamous loan shark had bled to death. That last shot had done for him.

By the time the police arrived, the bar was back to normal and apart from a dead body behind the curtains, nothing seemed amiss. Of course no-one had heard or seen anything. There was nothing to identify Kelly, his pockets having been emptied long before Mr Plod rolled up and Paddy Coyle had the key to his future securely tucked away.

Love at First Sight

Paddy approached a smart, end-terraced house on the outskirts of Glasgow, with well-kept gardens and a couple of cars in the drive. What the hell was he doing here? Why in God's name had he taken it upon himself to break the news to the family? He should be at the hospital with Sean and Michael, or at home with his ma and Marie. Christ, there would be ructions over this and there would be no living with her, now that one of her predictions had actually come true.

Hundreds of questions were racing around in his head. But the most important was, what the fuck was McClelland playing at? This was way out of his league. What could the arsehole gain by taking Micky out? Unless it was to gain control of his money-lending business, but that didn't make sense. He was in the wrong territory and every time one of his men stepped foot in the East End they would be shot. No, it just didn't make sense.

He hoped there was no-one home as he rang the bell, but the hall light came on and a young woman answered the door. Jesus, where did she fall from? She was fucking gorgeous, and for a minute he forgot why he was there. Stuttering and mumbling, Paddy was lost for words. How the fuck do you tell someone their da or husband has just been murdered, especially a creature like this? Fuck, what was he doing here?

"Can I help you?" she asked.

"Erm, I'm sorry to bother you, but I need to speak with Mrs Kelly, please," he managed to get out.

"You'll have a hard job," smiled the girl. "She left about twelve years ago, got a better offer so I heard. I'm Bridget Kelly. Why do you want my mother?"

"Oh, God, is there anyone else with you? A brother or sister, anyone?" He was way out of his depth.

"And why would you want to know who is at home? If you're a burglar or something, I'll set the dogs on you." At this point, a huge ginger cat waddled past on its way to the fireside.

"Mm, it must be Rover's night off," she laughed.

"I'm sorry, really I am, but it's your da," Paddy all but choked on the words.

"What about my father? What's the matter?"

"Look, can I come in? I'm not on the rob or anything. Is there a neighbour that could come?" he asked, hoping he could get this over quickly and be on his way.

"For God's sake, come in. You're starting to scare me." She led him into a warm, comfortable lounge.

Christ, crime certainly does pay, he thought, as he compared his shithole of a house to this place and Mad Billy Mitchell's.

"I think you should sit down, Miss Kelly, I've got bad news I'm afraid."

"Bad news? What's happened? Is it my father?"

"Look, I'm sorry, there is no good way of telling you, but Mickey passed away earlier tonight."

"Passed away? What, like a heart attack or was it an accident?"

"He was shot," replied Paddy, who was struggling to keep his mind on the reason he'd come and desperately trying not stare at this stunning female.

The young woman turned deathly pale. "Shot? You're telling me he was shot? I don't believe it. There's been some mistake. Who are you, anyway?"

"Miss Kelly, Bridget, I assure you there is no mistake. I work for your da. Sorry, worked for him, and I was there when it happened. The police will be here soon, you'll have to identify the body. Surely there's someone you could call on?"

"No, no-one. I'm fine, you can go. Thank you for your trouble, I'll be fine."

She looked like she was about to throw up at any second. Crossing the room to the drinks cabinet, Paddy poured the distraught young woman a large measure of brandy.

"Here, drink this," He handed her the glass and again quizzed her on her lack of family. "Have you definitely no relatives nearby?"

"No, they're all in Ireland and honestly, I haven't seen them in years. Dad kept himself to himself."

Paddy couldn't imagine having no-one. Mad as he got with his lot, they were close, and no matter what turned up, there would always be a shoulder to cry on. Not so for this gorgeous creature. He couldn't go and leave her, there had to be somebody.

"A boyfriend, mates, surely?"

Interrupted by the sudden ringing of the phone, Paddy poured another brandy for Bridget and one for himself, and by God he could do with it. He listened to the conversation which seemed to be from one of Kelly's collectors and certainly not the most sympathetic of mourners.

The caller, having confirmed the devastating news, was kindly offering to take care of her late father's business, as well as, of course, sending his condolences to the grieving family. The vultures were circling, even this quickly.

There was call after call from the dead man's ex-associates, each gravely sorry for her loss and anxious to assist in her hour of need. Well, as far as her father's clients were concerned, business was business, after all.

Paddy was extremely impressed with the way Bridget handled the grave robbers. This was not some shrinking violet; the girl could fend off threats without giving offence and with the promise to be in touch when and if she needed help, leaving each contender thinking he had won the prize. They all assumed she was a mug and Mickey Kelly's extremely lucrative business would soon be coming their way. Not if Bridget had anything to do with things, and unknown to her, even less if Paddy could help it.

It was almost 11pm when two police officers pitched up and curtly informed Miss Bridget Kelly that it appeared her father had been the victim of a gangland execution and she would be required to accompany them to the city morgue to identify the body.

Despite her being able to deal with the calls, a visit to the morgue at midnight was way more than Bridget could deal with. No matter what Paddy thought of Kelly, she was still his flesh and blood and the poor, grieving daughter had been completely traumatised by the evening's events.

"Miss Kelly will attend in the morning. She has to contact family members and her solicitor. Now, if you'll excuse us," Paddy showed the two reluctant officers to the door.

"It would be helpful if you could attend this evening," pressed one.

"Helpful to who?" countered Paddy.

"And you are?" questioned the first officer, recognising Paddy but unable to place him.

To this day, Paddy Coyle had no idea why, or if he actually did say, "Patrick Coyle, Miss Kelly's fiancé."

A loud gasp from Bridget almost gave the game away.

"Yes, I'm her fiancé and I'll bring her along in the morning. So, gentlemen, if you'll excuse us," Paddy ushered them out into the cold night and slammed the door before any further conversation could ensue.

"What the bloody hell did you go and say that for?" wept Bridget. "Look, you have to go, I can't get my head round all this and I'm sure you mean well, but you're making things worse."

"Do you really not have anyone that you can call, no-one anywhere?"

"How many times have I got to tell you? And not only am I not your fiancée, I'm not your problem. I can deal with this." Tears streamed down her cheeks.

Paddy was mesmerised by her. Always popular with the girls round his way, he had never had what anyone could call a serious relationship – family commitments and demands had put paid to that. Truthfully, he wasn't that interested, they were too much bother, but he'd never come across anyone like Bridget Kelly.

"Listen, girl, I wasn't your dad's favourite person and he certainly wasn't mine, but no way can I leave you to the mercy of the bastards he associated with. You've had a small taste tonight and believe me, this is only the beginning."

"And what's in it for you?" snapped Bridget.

"Oh, make no mistake, I'll have anything that's going, but I don't think you have any idea what's going to happen here. Before your da is cold in the ground all those vultures will be picking the meat clean off his bones. You'll be lucky to be left with the drawers you're standing in."

"I beg your pardon . . ."

"Listen to me, you're a woman on your own and no matter how smart you are, and you are smart, these fuckers will strip you clean. So if you want to come out of this with the price of a bus ticket to nowhere, go it alone. Otherwise, go and get some sleep and let me figure out what's to be done. And turn that fucking phone off."

The shock of what had happened finally hit her and the poor lass crumpled before his eyes. Realizing the enormity of the situation, Bridget was inconsolable. There was nothing Paddy could do but simply hold the girl till the sobs finally abated. She smelled so clean and fresh it was difficult for him to concentrate on why he was there.

Fuck, not exactly the time to be hitting on the poor bint, he chuckled to himself, well aware and a bit embarrassed about the effect she was having on him.

Identify

It was a long night, and the two strangers had talked and talked. Each settled on one of the comfortable sofas in the dimly lit room, warmed by the dying embers of the fire. Maybe it was the anonymity of the surroundings, but Paddy Coyle had never opened up to anyone in his life the way he did to Bridget Kelly during the wee small hours.

He told her about his errant father and all his madcap antics. How he, Paddy, felt, not knowing if the man was dead or alive, not a problem Bridget would have to face. He spoke of the responsibility he had in supporting his family at such a young age. About McClelland's treachery, deliberately omitting the fact that it was his ex-buddy who had pulled the trigger.

They even got round to how each saw their future. Paddy astounded himself by admitting he wanted a wife and family and maybe a house like the one they were in. To say that this shocked the young lad was an understatement. He had never given the future much thought, he was always too busy dealing with the present, but now that he'd voiced it out loud he realised it was exactly what he wanted, and ridiculously, he wanted the girl sitting opposite him to be a part of it.

Fuck! Am I going soft or what? I've only known her five minutes and we're walking down the aisle, Paddy laughed to himself.

"What's so funny?" she asked, drinking Paddy in. No man had ever had the effect that he was having on her.

God Almighty, I've just been told my father's dead and I'm desperate to cop off with his henchman. I've heard of don't shoot the messenger, but surely shagging him is just as bad?

It was sheer animal lust and both knew the inevitable would happen; it was just a question of when.

Bridget confided in Paddy of her fear and dislike of her father. He'd given her everything she could ever want and had never laid a hand on her, but she knew this was because she kept her mouth shut and did his bidding. There was no real father-daughter bond between them. She was his possession and if the day had ever come that he had no use for her, maybe she'd have disappeared like her mother had. God, where had that come from?

Her mother had run off, abandoned her without warning when she was only seven, on the day before her birthday. There had been no indication that there was anything wrong and there didn't seem to be anyone else. In fact, there had been no explanation at all. She was just gone. Bridget had cried herself to sleep night after night for a long time, and spent hours gazing out her bedroom window, waiting for her mum to come back, but she never did.

There was little Bridget didn't know about her father's business dealings or how he earned his money. She understood the fact that he had to operate under a cloak of secrecy so she was discouraged from having friends, 'just in case'. As for boyfriends, they all were seen off, either physically discouraged or threatened. Who the hell was going to put their life in jeopardy for a one night stand with her? After all, she was nothing special.

She was no fool and while she didn't condone what her father did for a living, it was simply a fact of her life. The reality was, she had expected the knock on the door for years and she admitted to Paddy it wouldn't be the first time she had actually prayed for it to come. She wanted a life and she was certainly no hypocrite.

Paddy woke to the tantalising smell of bacon wafting through the house. For a few moments he had no idea where he was. Then the previous evenings events came flooding into his head. What had he got himself into? Telling the boys in blue he was her fiancé. What a fucking eejit. The more he listened to Bridget, the more he realized she knew what was what. That still didn't make her fair game for her dad's mates. No, he was going to stick around for a bit, and not just for her sake, or so he told himself.

"How do you like your eggs?" she asked and quelled his usual reply of 'fertilized' with one look.

That one sentence, that one silly question, did it. Neither believed in love at first sight; that was for stupid women's magazines, wasn't it? Something had happened between them, no doubt about it. They were a couple, God knows how, but they were. Bridget knew from the bottom of her heart that he would take care of her and Paddy knew she was 'the one'. He would fight tooth and nail for her, protect and cherish her. Starting today. Yes, from now on they were in it together. What the fuck would his mother say?

The phone started its constant ringing again. The word was out on the street, there was a vacant spot to fill and everyone wanted a piece of it. Fortunately for Mickey Kelly's daughter, the dead man's 'bible' was missing. Without it there was no business, which meant a number of hungry villains were convinced that both Paddy and Bridget knew far more than they were letting on. There were also a lot of very relieved customers, many of whom were celebrating maybe just a tad too prematurely.

Consolidation

Four weeks after the funeral, Paddy and Bridget were married. It was a quiet affair with only Lizzie, the twins and Marie in attendance. The young couple had made it known that it was too soon after Mickey's death to be celebrating, but if the truth be told, there was no-one else to invite. Bridget had almost no relatives, certainly none who would go to the expense of attending a wedding, and the Coyles were such a self-sufficient quintet that they too were thin on the ground where family was concerned.

Police enquiries into the death of the local moneylender drew a blank on all counts. Little or no effort was made to trace the culprits, thanks to years of backhanders. There was virtually no chance of the perpetrator being apprehended and the case was unofficially closed. Micky Kelly's remains were released for burial in just less than three weeks. All the while the vultures were circling.

On the fourth day after the murder, Paddy had

produced the 'bible' and all her father's personal effects. His future wife had asked for no explanation and Paddy had given none, the understanding being that they were now on an equal footing and trusted each other implicitly. They were bound together for better or worse.

There was a no-expenses-spared, lavish funeral with the traditional black horses, glass carriage, and the usual accord given to a person of standing. This was done, of course, for the living, not the dead. Every 'face', or their representative, attended the Requiem Mass, conducted by the bishop himself. There was one notable absentee family: the McClellands. Uncle, nephew and foot soldiers were holding their own wake for their deceased in the famous Horseshoe Bar, together with their guest of honour, none other than Mad Billy Mitchell, recently released from hospital. Never a particularly handsome dude, Mad Billy was a queer-looking creature now, thanks to a certain person's handywork. The damage done to his right eye gave him a permanent look of surprise, together with the crisscross scars adorning his face. You wouldn't want to meet *him* on a dark night.

Never the most sociable of men, Mitchell was an even more bitter and twisted caricature of the man he'd once been. His motto, to anyone who would listen was, 'Don't get mad, get even.' And with the backing of his new buddies, that was exactly what he intended to do. But his was the long game and Paddy Coyle would keep. Mitchell would strike when he least expected it.

The official wake was held in the Gunners, the pub where Kelly had breathed his last and where Bridget carried out the grieving daughter duties to perfection. She received condolences from men who had hated and despised her father, but were anxious to keep in favour with the family, such as it was.

The whereabouts of the 'bible' and where it would turn up eventually was openly discussed. Mostly by those who'd owed substantial amounts of money and were, quite wrongly, under the impression that they had got off scot free. It came, therefore, as a major shock to those present when it was whispered that there was a new sheriff in town; it was soon to be business as usual and Paddy Coyle would be back on collections. More than a dozen mourners left town that day.

It transpired that Mickey Kelly had been far more astute than anyone had given him credit for, none more than his offspring. Bridget now owned the house she lived in, two others in Bearsden, a bookies shop where she had worked for a short time, and the 'bible'. All in all, she was a wealthy woman. Her wedding gift to Paddy was to hand everything over to him, lock, stock and barrel, with instructions to make as much money as he could, as quickly as he could, and then go legit. Bridget had no desire to live the life her father had created, but would tolerate it for the time being.

The Beginning of the End

"Oh my God, she's absolutely beautiful." Paddy gazed at the tiny bundle asleep in his arms. "Just like her mother," he kissed his wife gently on the cheek. "I'm so sorry, sweetheart. Honest, I got here as fast as I could."

"It's okay, Paddy. Really, it's okay. You're here now and that's what matters."

Bridget was worn out, she'd had a difficult birth, made all the more difficult by Paddy being AWOL, but she knew she shouldn't complain. After all, she was the one who had made the rules.

But his mother wasn't so forgiving. Lizzie clipped her big son round the ear, "Fecking missing at the birth of your first child, fecking disgrace. Whatever you said about your da, he was always there."

"Aye, maybe at the conception, but not always at the birth," said Sean, nodding towards Marie.

"Enough," Bridget quipped. "If I'm okay with it, then it's bugger-all to do with any of you lot."

"I can't believe how perfect she is," her daddy chuckled. She was only a few hours old and already she had him wrapped around her little finger.

"She's a beauty alright," said a proud and delighted Lizzie. "This one will break a few hearts when she gets older."

"No chance," her father joked. "They'll have to go through me first."

Those standing round the cot weren't so sure he was joking.

Erin had entered the world at 2.45 that morning, at the precise moment the life juices of one Jimmy McGregor had just expired, and Paddy Coyle had been responsible for both.

Almost a year had passed since Mickey Kelly's murder and Paddy Coyle was now more than something to be reckoned with in the hierarchy of the Glasgow criminal fraternity. His arrival on the scene had been met with great indignation and contempt.

To say Paddy met with opposition at taking over Kelly's businesses was putting it mildly. There were many would be 'faces' who were under the very wrong impression that they were entitled to a slice of the pie and in some cases, all of it.

Firms who had been sworn enemies for decades joined forces to eradicate this young pup. But the Coyle clan were too smart and too strong to be taken out of the picture. Their main strength lay in the fact that they were organised. Every aspect of their business had a strategy, a plan, and the plan was to be number one. Paddy was ruthless. He knew it was a 'them or us' situation and casualties were a fact of life or death.

His first action had been to sack every member of the Kelly firm. They were old, useless and skimming so much it was hardly worth collecting. They needed putting out to pasture. Most of the boys went without a fight, knowing they'd had it good for the past few years and who had no intention of bowing to this new boss. But there were a few die-hards, Kelly's top men, who thought they were worth more than a sweet goodbye and went out of their way to cause as much aggravation as possible, the last of whom was the aforementioned Jimmy McGregor.

McGregor had been with the firm since day one and had been instrumental in arranging the first ever loan. A loan that was, incidentally, still being paid off all these years later. He and Kelly had been mates from way back when. Nicking dinner money off their classmates had put paid to what little schooling either of them needed or wanted. They could read, write and count and that was enough for these two wide boys. Their first entry into the criminal world was via a (not very profitable) raid on a sub-post office. This had earned them a trip to court and a holiday, courtesy of Her Majesty, lasting six months.

Jimmy McGregor was adamant the 'bible' should be his. He'd worked it for Mickey Kelly for the past twenty years and knew every entry. There was no way he was bowing down to this fucking interloper, married to the daughter or not. The 'bible' was his, and he'd show them. With the help and assistance of his parish priest, McGregor managed to stay under Paddy's radar for almost a year and cause him all sorts of grief, much to the delight of Canon O'Farrell.

Paddy, together with the twins, had recruited a workforce from his neighbourhood, gym and a few he'd done time with. These boys were fit, drug-free, loyal and hungry. The rewards were second to none. Top of the range cars meant guys were clamouring to join the firm. His squad knew the score and on the morning after Mickey's funeral, a dozen or so baronial homes all over the city were petrol-bombed.

This was a warning shot over the bows that the Coyles meant business. Within the first week, every turf suffered casualties. Pubs, clubs and saunas were hit, causing panic and fury in every patch and a huge drop in business. Who was going to visit a sauna and get their bits blown off? These actions were costing money.

"Time to talk," he told the person on the other end of the line. "Two o'clock at the Horseshoe, you on your own, no guards and no shooters. Be there or suffer the consequences."

"Who the fuck do you . . .?"

"Two o'clock," and the dialling tone purred as Paddy disconnected.

Two calls were received by the most dangerous men in Glasgow; the term, drug barons was too insignificant.

Outside the Horseshoe Bar stretched a line of cars.

To the innocent passer-by it looked like some society funeral, which was a possibility. Each vehicle had two or three heavies primed and ready for action. At the other end of the spectrum, a few police officers were struck down with the 'skits' on what could turn out to be another Valentine's Day Massacre.

Paddy Coyle sat at the head of the table, a twin on either side. On the right, sat the infamous Mario Cortalessa, also known as 'The Italian'. He and his mob ruled the west of the city and governed using the laws of the Cosa Nostra. He was one scary, scary fucker.

First to speak was Davey Thompson from the north sector, the one man Paddy feared the most, not that he would ever let that be known.

"What the fuck is this all about?" asked Thompson. "Who do you think you are, summoning me like some fucking lackey?"

"You've got some fucking nerve, boy! Do you think lending a few quid to some housewives lets you play with the big boys?" said 'boss man' McIntosh. Nick McIntosh was the only out-of-towner invited. He was responsible for Paisley and all points west.

"Hey, you've made your mark, no doubt about it, but I could hit you so hard, fucking Lizzie would feel it."

It was true the Italian *was* scary and Paddy knew he was way out of his league.

"Where are McClelland and his boy?" asked Thompson. "Better things to do?"

"They were never invited," replied Paddy. "I've asked you here to make a deal. My men will back off, no more interruption to business, the turf remains the same and I operate Mitchell's patch."

"If we let you," sneered the Italian.

"You haven't stopped me doing exactly what I want so far and believe me, I have more manpower than you three put together. All young, all hungry, all ready to go to war."

"Are you threatening us, you stupid cunt? You do know you've just signed your own death warrant?"

The interconnecting doors slid open and revealed upwards of twenty men, armed, standing to attention, all ready for action; the war lords were fucked, each of them figuring this may well be their last breath.

"Do we have an agreement?" asked Paddy. "Shake on it and things go back to normal. The Coyles leave you alone."

Reluctantly, the men agreed to his proposals, shook hands and hightailed it out of the pub. This pup had turned out to be a snarling Doberman.

And now, here they were, a year down the line, well in control of the East End of Glasgow, with relative peace between them and the other firms, and the last of Kelly's henchmen had met his maker this morning. If the stupid old bastard had only taken his 'pension' and retired to sunny Benidorm like the rest of his mates, he'd still be alive. Not swaying at the bottom of Clyde in a pair of concrete boots.

The Coyles demanded absolute obedience and loyalty, neither of which had been big on McGregor's agenda, but his bête noir had been that he was related to the McClellands and blood will out.

He'd fucking haunt the bastard, was Jimmy's last thought before the water closed over him and silence reigned.

Tickling his daughter under her chin he reluctantly handed Erin back to her mother for a feed. Paddy swore to himself that he would never let anything, or anyone harm this precious bundle.

The Aftermath

"**B**uenos dias, Jose."

"Buenos dias, signor. Your guest is waiting in the office for you. I have taken his luggage to the villa."

"Gracias. I won't need you till later today, go help Sofia with the deliveries and make sure I am not disturbed for the next hour."

"Si, signor."

The small Spaniard loped off across the main floor of the club. Pete never failed to marvel at the opulence of the Marbella Princess, his latest acquisition. This place simply oozed glamour and decadence. This was not a club for the self-catering brigade. No, this was a club where a bottle of house champagne cost 400 euros and the bartender was likely to have appeared in some B-list movie. Every night was party night and every night the club was full to capacity. The latest DJs were flown in from all over Europe and for the first time in ten years Pete McClelland, or Pete

Mack, as he was now known, and his family felt safe.

"Buenos dias, Father, it's good to see you. Drink?"

Pete hated the priest intensely, but it was testament to his acting skills that Canon Francis O'Farrell had never twigged that his gracious host would shoot him without a second thought.

It was entirely down to this man that the McClellands were where they were today. They were multi-millionaires, friends with some of the most influential people in Europe and on first name terms with most of the UK's gangland chiefs who lived in the Costa Del Crime.

On the downside, they were exiled from home, had new identities and were separated from family and friends. Laughingly, Pete would joke that he would rather be exiled in Marbella than have the freedom of the city of Glasgow. There was the weather for a start!

"I'll show you round before you go up to the house," Pete offered. "It's been worth every penny and seriously, there's nothing that can compare with it in the whole of Europe. I've already had a couple of offers to buy me out."

"You've certainly come a long way since you were nicking coins out of the communion plate," laughed the old man. "No-one would ever recognise you as the petty thief I helped all those years ago."

Clenching his teeth, Pete let the remarks wash over him and joked away with Frank, as the priest liked to be known. The old bastard never let it go, always had to remind Pete of their history. But one day, Frank would get his comeuppance.

Dianne, Mack's wife of over twenty years was waiting up at the villa and she had a right cob on her, a face like a well-slapped arse. They had argued into the night about the impending visit, resulting in Dianne storming off to bed and Pete being faced with a locked bedroom door, not that that was any hardship.

It was the same every time the canon was due to visit. Dianne couldn't understand why Pete invited him to stay at the house in the first place. For fuck's sake, he wasn't family, he was nothing to them. If the truth be known, he gave her the bloody creeps, and once, years ago, when Bobby was just a toddler, she'd caught the dirty old bastard taking pictures of him. Oh, it was all explained away, but Dianne never forgot and made damned sure that the circumstances never happened again.

"Hello, dear, so nice to be back and you're looking wonderful as usual. I was just telling Pete here how well you've aged."

Dianne Mack had always been a looker and took extremely good care of herself. A little nip here, a bit of a tuck there and she was no stranger to the Botox needle. Yes, she was looking extremely good for her years, but she certainly didn't appreciate backhanded compliments from a fuckin' ancient, dried up priest, the bloody cheek of the man. Snorting something at both men, she called on Lucia the housekeeper to show Canon O'Farrell to his rooms. No way was she skivvying to him, let Mr Hospitality do the honours.

"Frank, my dear. Call me Frank, I'm a civilian this week."

"How long have we got you for this time?" growled Dianne.

"Just a week, I'm afraid. What a character, Pete, anyone would think I wasn't welcome. My dears, if I'm an imposition, just say the word. I wouldn't dream of putting you to any bother. I could just stay at the mission."

"Don't be daft, Frank; we're delighted to have you," Pete turned to his wife. "Aren't we, precious?"

"Fuck off, ya big woose. Dinner's at six tonight, take it or leave it." Dianne marched out to the pool where her son and his two mates were sunning themselves.

"What's up, Mum?" Bobby asked shading his eyes from the strong Spanish sun.

"Bloody Frank's just arrived, and your father's fawning around him like he's the fucking Lord Mayor. Why? What is the old fucker to us? Honestly, I just can't stand him and I've never understood why the hell your dad puts up with him."

"Don't get yourself in a state, I'll look after him and keep him out your way," offered Bobby. "I don't mind the old boy, he's quite funny at times."

"No you bloody won't, you keep well away from the old pervert."

She knew Bobby was safe enough now. Frank had lost interest in him years ago. It was definitely small boys he preferred, and it turned her stomach. She'd decided this was definitely going to be his last visit. It had gone on for years and Pete, who'd hardly ever been in a bloody church since he was baptised, was all of a sudden a fucking born-again Catholic.

Frank felt the warmth of the sun on his face as he stood on the terrace, watching Dianne and the boys with interest. She would be even unhappier if she knew what her husband got up to behind her back, chuckled Canon O'Farrell. That was a can of worms best left unopened. Where did she think all the money came from? You didn't get to own the Marbella Princess without some serious wedge.

Pete McClelland, with his wife and son, had arrived in Marbella with a couple of suitcases apiece and five thousand quid. Considering what they had left behind, this was petty cash. Pete needed to make money fast and he knew exactly how he was going to do it. It was a case of supply and demand. The demand was for human flesh, very young human flesh and he was more than prepared to supply. A few trips and he was in business. How did the good father fit into this enterprise? The confessional, coupled with a damned good memory.

At the beginning of his ministry in Craigloch there had been a number of attacks on toddlers, mainly little girls. The attacks were quite random and all the evidence pointed to a poor 'soft' lad called Thomsie Curran. He was a boy from the flats who was fifteen, but with the mental age of a four-year-old, whom the other kids teased mercilessly, all except for Pete McClelland. Pete was Thomsie's only friend. A strange combination, but Thomsie followed McClelland everywhere.

Father O'Farrell had never believed Thomsie was responsible and had protested his innocence to all and sundry. In fact, at the time of one particular incident, the boy had actually been with him. Unfortunately for Thomsie, Father O'Farrell couldn't own up. He'd be in jail, de-frocked and excommunicated if this dalliance ever came to light.

Worse still, poor Thomsie was set upon by a crowd of women from the neighbourhood, a virtual lynch mob, who made sure he would never carry out anything of the like again.

The attacks stopped, but only for a short while, too late to help Thomsie. Father Francis O'Farrell was not a man who suffered remorse or guilt for any of his actions. He conveniently cited God as the reason things had to be done, bar the one incident. He regretted the treatment doled out to poor Thomsie Curran and the distaste in which the neighbourhood still held him.

It came as no surprise years later, when Pete McClelland's penchant for little girls came to the good father's attention that Pete's Spanish import/ export business gained a silent partner.

Sound of Silence

"This is your Captain speaking, welcome aboard Flight BA345 to Malaga. We are now cruising at 50,000ft and the outside temperature is -40 degrees. Our estimated time of arrival is 12.08 . . ."

Erin was ecstatic, two weeks of freedom; she still couldn't believe she'd managed to pull it off. Here she was, actually airborne with the girls, drinking a vodka and coke and trying to open one of those piddly little bags of nuts. She was so excited she'd almost wet herself when the flight took off, convinced up until then that at some point Big Paddy would storm the plane and drag her back home. But no, she was flying high and boy was she going to make up for lost time. Two weeks with no mother fussing over her and no dad checking her every movement, unbelievable!

She had begun her 'Marbs' campaign way back on New Year's Day. The best day of the year in every Scottish home and Erin knew if she were to succeed with her plan this was the day to plant the seed. All the family was gathered for the traditional New Year dinner. Grannie Lizzie and her uncles looked a bit green around the gills, having been 'First Footing' till God knows when. Surprisingly, they were all in fine fettle, despite having spent a lazy afternoon drinking the finest malt whisky and reminiscing about the old days when a 'face' was a 'Face', not some fucking Russian oligarch, shipping drugs and sex workers into the UK by the boatload.

How different from when Paddy and the twins had started out in the business. First of all, the big man had had to fight his way through the ranks, and there were some real hard fuckers in Glasgow then. Not like the 'office boys' now, with their spreadsheets and world wide web. Back then, fleets of ice-cream vans had carried almost all the contraband round Glasgow and the drivers fenced anything from a nuclear sub to a five pound baggy. It was an ingenious setup and had worked for years until the turf war broke out. Drivers crossing over into other territories, gang bosses getting greedy and the filth costing so much to quash investigations, the whole system had imploded in on itself and changed Glasgow forever.

"You okay, sweetheart?" Her mum mouthed from the other side of the room.

"No, not really," the girl signed back to her. "I want to talk to you about something," her fingers spelled out the words.

"Help me clear the table and we can have a chat." Bridget stroked her daughter's hair affectionately.

She was so proud of Erin. Despite her handicap the

girl had overcome it, never letting it stop her doing anything. Whatever the problem, Erin found a way round it.

Since the horror of her First Holy Communion, Erin Coyle had lost the power of speech. The shock and trauma of the shootings had literally rendered the little girl speechless. Paddy and Bridget had been distraught and taken the girl to every specialist in the country. They had travelled to Europe and even to the U.S., to no avail. Every single physician had come up with the same diagnosis: Chronic Dysphonia, and every one without exception had predicted that at some point in Erin's life the condition could reverse itself. But there was no known cure and no guarantees.

Time after time the parents were told the same thing. Paddy blamed himself. Almost eighteen years ago he had promised his daughter, on the day she was born, that he would always be there for her and he would never let her down. Despite Bridget's assurances, Paddy would not be placated. He had failed his family and if it took till his dying breath he would have revenge.

After the initial trauma, Erin had adjusted, as most children do, unlike her parents. She learned to sign, as did her classmates and teachers. Surprisingly quickly, she fell into a fairly normal routine. If you could call having a father like Paddy Coyle normal, then that's what she had. She knew, even after all these years, he was still on the lookout for those who'd been the cause of her silence.

"What's wrong, chicken?" asked Bridget.

"I want you to ask Dad for something," she signed.

"Ask him yourself," laughed her mother. "You've more chance of getting round him than I have."

"Not for this."

"Okay, what's the mystery? What do I have to ask for that you won't?" puzzled Bridget.

"I want to go on holiday with the girls, Mum. A break before we all go our separate ways."

"Erin, he won't let you go, not on your own. You know why."

"But Mum, I'll be eighteen next month. I don't want any stupid party. I want to go away on holiday like everyone else. I'm not a kid and I promise you, I'm going – with or without his permission."

"Without whose permission?" interrupted her dad, entering the room.

Years of having to think on her feet in order to avoid trouble helped Bridget to blatantly lie to her husband without batting an eyelid.

"It's just a school trip. Erin was saying she doesn't need to get signed permission."

"Oh, she still has to get mine, though," smiled Paddy, "wherever she's going."

A look passed between mother and daughter; now was not the time to ask. Better she should get everyone on her side before she broached the subject with her father.

Later on in the day she cornered the twins, she loved her uncles and knew they would do almost anything for her, even tackle her dad.

"What's up kid, you seem very quiet today?"

"In case you hadn't noticed, I'm always quiet," Erin quipped back.

"Smart-arse," Sean laughed at her.

"Okay, what do you want us to do, what will daddy not give in about?"

"How do you know I want you to do anything? Can't I just be nice to my two favourite uncles?"

"For a start, we're your only uncles, and you, madam, are only nice to us when you want something, right Sean?"

"Right, Michael."

"So what is it then?"

With all the drama that an eighteen-year-old could muster, Erin made them promise they would talk her dad into letting her go off with her friends. Not that they held out much hope, but for her they'd give it a try.

Next, the girl talked Granny Lizzie onto her side, but her biggest ally was Auntie Marie, the wild child no longer. Like Erin, the trauma of the communion party still affected Marie all these years later.

Paddy's sister had been in intensive care for weeks after the shooting. The family had never left her side – she had been at death's door on more than one occasion. The medics had all but given up on her, but she was a Coyle and miraculously, she survived. Her injuries left her paralysed down her right side and the prognosis for the young woman was not good. Everyone was resigned to the fact she would be confined to a wheelchair for the rest of her life, all except Paddy. He was determined she would recover, and with sheer grit and fortitude she proved the doctors wrong. Marie Coyle was cut from the same cloth as her brothers.

She and her son Errol still lived at 28 Lomond Gardens with Lizzie. Unfortunately, her brush with death had not cultivated her maternal instincts any and she was, as she told everyone, still a crap mother. However, fortunately for Errol, his nanny Lizzie and his uncles adored him and between them the boy flourished. Now aged ten and a quarter, a right little bugger, a handsome, coffee-coloured devil who could charm the birds from the trees.

Although knowing full well she wouldn't win Mother of the Year, Marie had no intentions of existing on handouts from her brothers. It was her job to provide for her son, and provide she would. Her options, however, were somewhat limited. Surely there was a place for her in the business? If she had to, she'd sweep floors, clean toilets, whatever, but she needed to earn a living.

She badgered her brothers daily to give her a chance and against Paddy's better judgement and Lizzie's disapproval, he allowed Marie to learn the ropes of his adult entertainment business. Quite frankly, no-one expected much from her, but she took to the business like a duck to water, amazing everyone, herself included. Running the saunas and lap dancing clubs was child's play to her. In her time there were few sins Marie hadn't committed and she'd seen and done the lot.

Under her supervision the profits doubled and she ran the establishments with a rod of iron. If the girls thought they were going to get an easy ride with her in charge, they had guessed wrongly. Marie was good, she had no favourites, everyone was a winner and her young niece loved her to death.

The Coyles were now well established. Over the years Paddy had sold off his fleet of vans and had acquired a couple of scrapyards, which were ideal for the car business and the disposal of anything incriminating. Coyle Security employed almost two hundred doormen and security guards, which provided the most valuable inside information on most of the illegal activities around the city. But his family's safety was the most important thing to Paddy. He would never leave them open to harm again. His mother Lizzie refused point blank to move from Craigloch. She had lived there for nearly forty years and had no intention of moving, declaring to all and sundry she would leave the house feet first. Now, unknown to her, the house was under 24 hour surveillance. Paddy saw no point in owning the biggest security firm in the city and his mother being unprotected. Paddy knew she'd have a fit if she found out, but it was a risk worth taking.

Bridget and Erin were a different matter. A substantial farm house in the country, a mere five miles from the city centre, also with 24 hour surveillance, was home to the Coyles and the big man played lord of the manor to the hilt.

Like a Virgin

The girls ran barefoot through the villa, bagging their rooms. Of course Kirsty had the master suite; after all, it was her family's property. There were two other suites and a smaller room on the other side of the terrace.

"If you're not fast, you're last," yelled Fiona, bagging the second biggest room which led straight out to the pool.

"This one's mine," squealed Lucy dumping her luggage next door. "Hey, Coyle, you're on a sun lounger," she joked with Erin who looked forlornly at her pals.

Signing, "Where am I going to sleep? I'm not really on a lounger, am I?"

"Don't be daft, you idiot, you're over the other side of the terrace. Nice and private, so don't go sneaking any boys back here."

"As if," Erin sneered.

She could still hardly believe she was off the leash.

Ironically, it was Auntie Marie, the ex-wild child who had swung the trip for her.

All through January and February, the twins, Lizzie and Bridget had tried their best to persuade Paddy to let the girl go away with her schoolmates, but he was having none of it.

"Why not Paddy? She's a sensible lassie." asked Lizzie time and time again. "Let her go, she's worked hard getting all them certificates and a place at university. Christ, no-one in this family ever got further than their eleven plus and even at that, no bugger passed."

Sean and Michael broached the subject a couple of times, but seeing their brother's reaction, gave it up as a bad job. Paddy was adamant, there was no way he was letting his princess off on her own, unsupervised. It wasn't that he didn't trust her, absolutely not; it was others he didn't trust. His little girl was a stunner: tall, standing at 5' 8" with long chestnut curls, skin like porcelain and a figure to die for, and completely unaware of the effect she had on the opposite sex.

Over the past couple of years he'd smacked God knows how many men, most of whom were his workforce, for daring to look at her in what he considered to be an inappropriate way. But it was Marie who challenged her older brother over the holiday. At the celebration dinner for Erin's eighteenth birthday (parties were a no-go in the Coyle household) and seeing her niece's downcast demeanour, Marie took the bull by the horns.

"You're a bloody fool, Paddy Coyle," she faced up to him over the table "A bloody fool."

"Is that a fact, sis? Maybe you should cut back on the old vino collapso," he countered, steeling himself for a set-to with his younger sister. He knew the signs and, restaurant or no, she'd have her say. What was her beef about this time?

"For a start, this is water," holding up the glass. "You are one stubborn stupid eejit. Think back to when I was eighteen."

"God forbid, you were a right little tearaway. There was no controlling you, was there?"

"No, but you bloody well tried hard enough. The word control, Paddy. That's what this is all about," cajoled Marie.

"Listen, my girl, you did exactly what you liked, when you liked and with whom you liked, the evidence of that is sitting at the end of this table."

"Oh, is that right? Well, if you don't let *her* out of her gilded cage, there might well be another cuckoo sitting at the end of the table quite soon. Think on."

"Who the fuck died and made you boss? So you're telling me if I stop my daughter going off to Spain with three brainless hussies she'll end up like you, running a strip joint with a ten-year-old bastard tucked up at home?"

There was a stunned silence. Nobody could quite take in what he had just said. Every person sitting round the table was shocked to the core, appalled. Sean jumped up but was pulled back by his twin.

"Leave this to Ma," he instructed his brother. "This is her shout."

Lizzie stood up and drawing herself to her full height, all of five feet, she walloped her eldest son round his ear. The last time she'd struck him was over ten years ago.

"My God, I can't believe what I've just heard. Never did I ever think I'd see the day when one of my sons would turn on his sister and say the things you just did. Let me tell you something, my lad, you will never, ever get the chance to insult any of mine again," And she turned to the rest of the family and ordered them to leave.

Paddy was gobsmacked, of course he hadn't meant to call Errol a bastard, he loved the kid, but who the fuck did they think they were? Telling him how to bring up his family.

Now alone at the table, he pondered on what had just happened. He was unaware that his daughter had come back into the dining room as he wiped the tears from his face. All he ever wanted was to keep them safe, all of them. Why could nobody understand that?

"I won't go, Dad, not if it causes so much trouble. I just wanted to have fun with the girls before getting down to studying. But we won't talk about it again. I'll come with you and Mum."

He looked at his daughter and knew he was going to have to give in. They were right, he had to let her grow up, but he had meant it, he didn't want her to have the life that Marie had, but he couldn't live Erin's life for her.

"Get me the numbers of the other parents and all the details and I'll think about it, no promises, mind." Rubbing his ear, he grinned at his girl, "She can still pack a punch, the old fucker."

Forever Hold Your Peace

Bobby Mack stood for a few minutes watching the four girls cavorting around in the water, pondering which one would be his playmate this week. They were all lookers, but in his world, a world populated by good-looking rampant females all up for fun, he was always spoilt for choice.

Being a pool boy was not exactly the dizzying heights his folks aspired to, but there was no telling him. At twenty-one, Bobby and his two best mates had started their own pool maintenance company to earn a bit of pocket money. Little did any of them perceive what a roaring trade they would drum up, so much so that they now had four other guys on the books; the main criteria being that they had to be fit and hung like a burro. They soon became the darlings of the Marbella set – you were no-one if you didn't have the best-looking pool guys in town taking care of your needs and maintaining the pool as well!

The boys had access to all the pussy they could

handle; bored wives who were spending the summer in Marbs or even posher Puerto Banus, while their husbands earned the money to keep them in style. Bank jobs, building society heists, a quick trip over to Tangiers to pick up a shipment or two, were all in a day's work for many of the inhabitants of the fashionable Spanish resort and for Bobby and his co-workers, it simply meant more money to be spent on them. Lotharios? Gigolos? Most definitely.

The music was deafening and the crowded club was heaving to the sounds. In the VIP area, Erin was signing to her girlfriends.

"Imagine the pool guys having VIP passes. Do you think they're genuine? Hope we don't get thrown out."

"They seemed to be well known. They went straight to the head of the queue and the doorman called him Mr Bobby. Maybe they work here as well." said Kirsty. "Anyway, Bobby's mine, so hands off, you can share the others," laughed Erin's friend.

"Hey, I'm not fussed. They're all dishy," squealed Fiona.

"Drinks, girls? Champagne, shots, cocktails, what are we having?" Bobby asked, summoning a waiter.

Even in the VIP area he snapped his fingers and immediately someone came running. Erin was fascinated. The pool guy was seriously good-looking and very charming. Okay, there were a few other lookers in the roped-off area, but none had his ability to get served, she laughed to herself.

The drinks arrived, bottles of champagne complete

with fireworks, glasses lined up with measured shots, and a selection of cocktails. No money changed hands; he was obviously well-known enough to have a tab. Erin had been brought up around bars and night clubs, she could spot a scammer a mile off; this was no rip-off merchant. The guy *was* well-known and clearly had money to burn; cleaning pools was obviously a very well paid job.

Bobby was not used to getting the brush off, especially in his father's club. Most girls, even the sophisticated ones, were well impressed by his VIP status in the Princess and literally threw themselves at the posse. Not so this one. He'd spoken to her a couple of times during the course of the evening, but nothing. She either just ignored him or shrugged her shoulders, no conversation, no interaction; she seemed only interested in the action down on the main floor. He was not at all impressed. Apart from anything else, he'd stood them drinks all evening; a simple thank you would suffice, but nothing, not a cheep.

Out on the dance floor he shouted to Fiona, "What's with your stuck-up mate?" It was difficult to hear and it took him a few minutes for Fiona to understand.

"Which one?" she queried, none of them having ever before been accused of being stuck-up. The girls were full of fun and nonsense, no matter where they went.

"Erin."

"Erin? Erin's not stuck-up, maybe a bit shy, but never stuck-up." Of course, being so familiar with her friend's disability, Fiona gave no thought to the fact that because Bobby and his sidekicks couldn't sign, Erin had no way to communicate with them.

"She's a snooty little mare," persisted Bobby. "I've spoken to her two or three times and nothing, she just shrugs her shoulders, smirks but doesn't deign to answer. I'm obviously just the hired help."

Fiona looked aghast at him. "You've got it all wrong. She can't speak, Bobby. I thought you'd realised this afternoon. I'm so sorry, Erin's brilliant, great fun and the least stuck-up person you could ever meet. She'll be devastated you thought that about her."

"What do you mean she can't speak? Everybody can speak." he bounced back at her.

"*She* can't. Her hearing's fine so she would know what you were saying, but she lost the power of speech when she was a kid, some kind of accident."

"Oh my God, what a bloody shame. And I'm going on about her not saying thank you for a fucking drink, what an arse," the young guy was really quite upset.

Marching into the VIP area, Bobby grabbed the silent girl by the arm and took off into the crowd. The music was deafening and like every other couple on the floor they could only communicate by gestures and pointing, for once it was a level playing field. She actually had an advantage over the other clubbers.

They eventually made their way back to the table, sweating profusely. By this time Fiona had given up on Bobby and was draped around Jake, snogging the face off him and not the least bit interested in their return. The other two exhibitionists were high up on the podiums and refusing to come down.

Dawn was breaking as the girls strolled, shoes in hand, back to the villa. What a night, Erin thought, what a night. She might just be a little bit in love.

Game Play

"You're just jealous," she furiously signed with great dramatic gestures. "Just jealous that it's me he wanted to be with."

"Don't be daft, Erin, nobody's jealous of you. It was obvious he fancied you from day one, so what's to be jealous of?" said Kirsty. The four girls were lounging round the pool when the argument broke out.

"I just thought since it was our last night we should spend it together," insisted Fiona. "The time has just flown by and you've been off with Bobby most of the holiday, we've hardly seen you."

"So? Anyway, who said it was my last night?"

Erin was definitely her father's daughter, the stubborn set of her chin and the defiance in her eyes spoke volumes. This was not the meek, self-effacing girl who'd landed in Spain more than a week ago. No indeed, this was a bird of a different feather altogether.

"What do you mean, not your last night?" laughed Lucy.

"Just what I said. It may be not my last night, I might stay on for a bit."

"Stay where? You can't stay here. My grandparents are coming out next week," said Kirsty.

"This isn't the only villa in town. Bobby's out looking for somewhere right now."

"Erin, it's a holiday romance. Enjoy it, but don't take it seriously, he'll be off with someone new before we've even cleared the duty free and got to the departure lounge."

"That's what you think. He won't. He's asked me to stay and he wants us to be together."

"That's what he'll say to all the girls, the guy's a player. He'll say it because he knows you can't stay and he's quite safe. Surely you're not falling for that old chestnut?"

"NO. No, No you're wrong," Erin signed. "We're going to get a place together and I'll get a job."

"Oh, how easy is that going to be? For Christ's sake, Erin, it's not only that you can't speak the language, but that you can't fucking speak," yelled Fiona.

"Hey, come on, that was a bit nasty, was it not?" Lucy turned on Fiona.

"Well, can you see our little princess mopping floors?" Lucy beseeched her friend. "Or cleaning toilets, 'cos those are the only jobs she'll be offered."

"Whoa there, this is getting way out of hand," Kirsty stood up. "Let's all calm down and sort this out properly without any more arguments."

"You sort it out for yourselves, I'm off. And don't wait up," Erin marched off into the villa.

"This needs to be sorted. We can't let her just walk out and maybe not come back. We need to get to Bobby. Kirsty, you must have his number somewhere, phone him."

Bobby Mack rolled up within the hour to be met by three very unhappy Glasgow girls. Meanwhile, Erin, completely unaware that her soulmate had just arrived and was being royally grilled by her best friends, was off in a fantasy realm. Examining herself in the mirror, she was sure she looked different, sure that the others had guessed and that's what the argument had really been about. She and Bobby had slept together the previous night. Well, not exactly slept together. They were both pretty pissed and had ended up getting carried away on the beach. Not exactly the way she had planned it, and certainly not the most romantic way of losing her virginity, but she was determined to more than make up for it tonight. Now, if she could just get the other girls out of the way.

"What do you mean she's not going home tomorrow?" asked Bobby. "Is she planning on staying on here?" He indicated the villa.

"No chance, my grandparents are arriving on Sunday so there's no way she can stay on, but that's not the point, she thinks you're going to live together in some fancy apartment."

"Shut up!"

"I'm telling you, she thinks you're out looking just now and the two of you are going to live happily ever after."

"Come on, she's a great girl and we've had an amazing time but that's it, I'm off. I'm strictly the 'love 'em and leave 'em' type, so you lot can say my goodbyes and have a safe journey home."

"Not a chance, mister. You can do your own dirty work and trust me, you better let her down gently, she's had enough trauma in her life, so you do what you have to do, but sort it."

"Sorry, I'm off." Bobby got up to leave just as Erin appeared in the doorway.

"Oh, you're early. That's okay, I'm ready, so we can go now," Erin smirked at the threesome.

"Sorry Babes, change of plan. I have to take a trip, family business, and I'm going to be away for a few weeks."

"But Bobby, what about us? What am I going to do while you're away?"

Kirsty had to translate all of this to Bobby who was squirming; really uncomfortable. This boy didn't do farewells and he couldn't wait to get away.

"Erin, this is family business and it comes before anything."

"You don't have to tell her about family business," quipped Fiona.

114

"No, Erin knows all about family business. Well, she should, seeing as she's a Coyle."

"A Coyle as in Paddy Coyle?"

"He's her dad."

"Well, you'll know what family means then. Listen, I've got your number. I'll be in touch, honest." And he jumped into his car and zoomed off.

"Why did you have to spoil everything? Why couldn't you leave things alone?" The poor girl was distraught, inconsolable, and nothing would placate her. A seriously miserable end to what should have been a fabulous holiday.

Bobby tore up the steps to the terrace, calling at the top of his voice for his father. He found him and Frank deep in conversation.

"Dad! Sorry Frank, but I have to speak to my dad alone."

Pete had seldom seen his son so agitated. "That's okay, son, you can speak in front of Frank."

"No. I need to speak to you on your own."

"No problem," said the priest, leaving father and son to discuss whatever was bothering Bobby. No doubt a female, smiled the old man. That boy's too handsome for his own good.

"Shit, Dad, I think I've brought trouble to us. Real trouble."

"How? What could you have done to get this upset?"

"I've just dumped Paddy Coyle's daughter, that's what, and after plucking her cherry."

"Hey, good for you, son," Pete laughed. "Revenge certainly couldn't be sweeter, but what's all the panic for?"

"I sort of promised her we'd be together always and all that guff. It's what I tell them all, but this daft bint believed me and is threatening all sorts, including topping herself."

"So let her. It's not your fault the stupid fool got taken in, and I can't see Paddy Coyle coming hightailing it over here to exact retribution for his daughter's virginity. Naw, you're fine, don't worry about it."

"Sure?"

"Of course I'm sure. Shame, really. If I'd known earlier I might have arranged a little something for Mr Coyle's precious daughter."

"Frank, come back in here a moment," Pete called to the priest who had been hovering in the vicinity.

"So he's just dumped Erin Coyle? There's a turn up for the books. Never thought she'd be let out of her gilded cage," smiled the priest. "You know he blames you for her condition."

"Me?" questioned Pete. "What condition and what did I do?"

"Surely you heard what happened to Erin on the day of her Holy Communion? My God, it must be ten years ago."

"Well, I know I got the blame for all the trouble, but for once it wasn't the McClellands. And I do know there was no time to stand and argue my case and stay alive. So what happened to her?"

"You know she can't talk?" Bobby asked his father.

"She can't talk? You're joking." interjected Pete. "But what's that got to do with me?"

"Well, she never said another word from that day on. They've had her to every specialist and they all say the same, she might regain her speech, but after this length of time it's doubtful."

"So? I still don't understand. Why's it my fault?"

"He thinks you mounted the attack and the outcome was that the girl lost the power of speech, so therefore, you are to blame."

"Fuck, I thought he just wanted what was mine, not that he was blaming me for what happened to his daughter. And it's taken almost ten years for me to find out about this?"

Farewell

Erin had sobbed her heart out all night. As far as she was concerned, her life was in ruins. She didn't want to live, she didn't want to stay in Spain, but the thought of putting all those miles between her and Bobby was even worse. There was nothing her friends could say or do to make things better; she was taking it really badly.

"This is what comes of being mollycoddled," said Fiona. "They've kept her so bloody wrapped up, the first guy that shows her any attention, down she goes, hook line and sinker."

"Hey, come on, he's not just any guy now, is he?" quipped Kirsty. "Neither of you would kick him out of bed."

"Talking of bed, do you think she did it?" queried Lucy.

"Oh, God. I hope not, but he's definitely not the type to waste his time, if you know what I mean."

"Naw, she's not that stupid, is she?" replied Lucy.

"Depends how much she had to drink or how persuasive he was."

"Hey, that's her problem. Let's get moving, we've got a flight to catch."

The girls did her packing for her, bundled her into a shower, managed to get her dressed and somehow they got to the airport. How things had changed in such a short time.

Having checked in, Erin hung back and surveyed the busy airport, hoping against hope that maybe . . .

"You three go on, I'll catch you up. I want a magazine."

"How stupid do you think we are? As soon as we're out of sight, you'll make a break for it."

"Erin, I know this is harsh but forget him. Trust me, he's already onto this week's lucky hot pick. You had a great time, with a fab looking guy and now it's back to reality."

"Fiona's right, for God's sake, pull yourself together. Do you think we've not all had our hearts broken? Just remember the good bits."

"Are you telling us you really want to tie yourself down at your age? Rubbish! All that housework, babies and everything that goes with it?"

"C'mon, this time next week it'll just be a distant memory."

With a slight tremor and a faint smile, Erin knew she had to go home, but hoped, just hoped, that he would come charging across the concourse and whisk her away.

*

119

"Dear God, look at the reception committee," Fiona caught sight of the crowd of people waiting outside the arrival hall.

"Shit! Can you imagine what would have happened if we'd turned up without her?" whispered Kirsty.

"Fuck, we'd all be floating in the Clyde," replied Lucy.

"Yeah, and everybody we know with us."

At the sight of her parents, uncles and granny, Erin burst into tears and was swept away in a bevy of concerned relatives.

"I told you I shouldn't have let her go," growled Paddy to anyone listening. Turning to her three companions, "Well, what's wrong? What's happened?"

The three girls didn't know what to say and it didn't look like Erin was going to come to their rescue.

"She's not been feeling well the last couple of days, Mr Coyle. I don't think the food agreed with her," ventured Kirsty. "And of course, she was terribly homesick."

That was exactly the right thing to say to Paddy Coyle, who was convinced, his family could not exist without him in their immediate vicinity.

"Okay, I trust you took good care of her?"

"Of course," the threesome chimed together.

"Sean, see these three young ladies get home, will you?" Paddy swept majestically out to his waiting car, vowing that this was his princess's first and last time away from the family.

The girls breathed a huge sigh of relief and silently

got into the waiting limo, well aware that they had got off by the skin of their teeth. Paddy Coyle was one scary man.

If it Sounds Too Good

Sitting in the warmth of the kitchen at Number 28, Lizzie and Marie were discussing Erin, and not for the first time either.

"What the bloody hell is going on there?" questioned Lizzie. "I can't make head nor tail of her lately. Dear Lord, if she's not sobbing her heart out, she's taking the feckin' face off you. I've never seen the likes, well, not with her, anyway."

"I've hardly seen her," Marie answered her mother. "If I didn't know better, I'd say she was avoiding me, but why? Hey, if it wasn't for me she wouldn't have gotten to go. So why the hell has she taken the hump with me?"

"God knows, hen, but something happened when she was away, that's for sure. Feckin' home-sickness. She's been home more than a month and still suffering from it. Bollocks, absolute bollocks."

"I'm telling you, she's met someone, as sure as apples are apples. I bet the silly mare has fallen for some sleazy Spanish waiter and is pining for him. I'm telling you, Ma, it'll be a bloke. It always is."

"Naw, she's never been much interested."

"She's never been allowed to," answered Marie.

"That's true, but how have that dozy pair not cottoned on? Let's face it, they know everything else about the lass."

"But that's the problem, the poor wee bugger is smothered. They do everything but breathe for her and it's not healthy. Fuck, we all know what happened the last time he left them alone. But for Christ's sake, Ma, if I can get over it, so can Erin."

"Don't ever let either of them hear you saying that, Marie, or you'll never hear the end of it. But you're right, they do smother her and it will end in more tears. Believe me, she's hiding something and I for one am not looking forward to finding out what."

Erin was well aware the family were worried, but for the life of her, she couldn't shake off her desolation. Friends called for her and she refused to see them. She missed parties and outings; she was just plain miserable, with no interest in anything.

She was about to start university in a few weeks, something she'd planned and worked hard at for years, but it now held nothing for her. She had no appetite and no matter what her mother or granny served up to her, it ended up in the bin. The girl was a shadow of her former self and for the first time in a long while, the fact she couldn't speak had become a big issue for everyone, especially her dad.

Paddy was beside himself with remorse. He should

have stuck to his guns and kept her at home, despite the mutterings of his wife and mother, and especially that bloody sister of his. Why in God's name had he ever listened to her of all people? Paddy Coyle was convinced that he, and he alone, could protect his family and yet again he'd let Erin down by giving in to this holiday malarkey.

He had that sick feeling in the pit of his stomach. He knew there was much more to this than bloody food poisoning and missing home, and he certainly wasn't the eejit his mother and sister seemed to think. But what was wrong? Boyfriends? He didn't think so, and there certainly had been no mention of anyone in particular. But by fuck, if anyone had been taking liberties with his princess, God help them. Paddy Coyle would do murder without a second thought.

Fresher's week should have been a round of drink, parties and fun, and Erin Coyle would always have been first up for a laugh and a good time. Now she dragged herself from lecture to lecture and then locked herself up in her room on the pretext of studying. In fact, she never opened a book, and as for the lectures, they could have been in a foreign language for all the attention she paid. Not only was she miserable, she felt awful, really ill. She was beginning to think there was something drastically wrong. Was she dying? In a sad way she hoped so. Then he'd be really sorry. It didn't matter what she ate or drank, up it came. And the more tempting the food, the worse she felt. If this was what a broken heart did, she would never look at another man in her life.

As she lay in bed, staring at the ceiling, Erin played over and over in her mind's eye the time she had spent with Bobby. Could he really have been lying about how he felt? Was it all just to get into her pants? Probably, but she would have let him anyway. He didn't need to lie. Was he saying the same things to some other girl right now? Probably.

She knew she had to pull herself together, but she just didn't know how. This was a girl who barely ever caught a cold, was always brimming with good health, she rarely even suffered from PMT.

Oh, fuck.

Sickness, feeling like death warmed up, and she couldn't remember when she'd last had her period, it was well before she went on holiday. She couldn't be, could she? They'd only done it once. Oh my God, her father would kill her. Yes, he would seriously kill her. What the hell was she going to do?

Pregnant Pause

Erin grabbed her purse and car keys and headed out. She couldn't wait, she had to find out now.

"Where are you off to, missy? I'm just about to serve lunch, your dad wants to eat now, he's got some meeting or other to attend," Bridget called after her daughter.

Erin slammed the door behind her.

"So much for family lunch," muttered Bridget to herself. There was something up with that girl and she hoped that what she suspected wasn't true. There would be murders in this house if she was right. She couldn't get hold of Erin long enough to get to the bottom of things, but she would.

Erin had no option but to go into town. The ladies in the village chemist knew her and the family well. There was no way a pregnancy test would go unnoticed or unannounced. Her mother would know about the purchase before she had the wrapping paper off.

God, if she had felt grim before, it was nothing to the way she was feeling now. She was ill with worry. How could this have happened? Surely it was an old wives tale. Only *she* was unlucky enough to get caught the first time. Unbelievable! Bloody hell, what was she going to do? No way could she confess to her mother. Her dad? Oh my God, forget it. She daren't even contemplate his reaction. What about her granny? Naw, she'd be just as bad. Marie, Auntie Marie. She'd help her, but first things first, maybe she was just late. It could be a false alarm. Perhaps the flight had knocked her system to hell, or the Spanish food hadn't agreed with her, or maybe just the misery of a broken heart? Who was she kidding? Talk about clutching at straws – she knew, deep down she knew.

Disappearing into the ladies powder room in Lewis's, she carried out the instructions. It seemed to be the longest five minutes of her life. Two blue stripes. Oh, fuck! Fuck, fuck, fuck. She gave it another try and five minutes later there were another two stripes. No doubt about it. She was in the club, up the duff, had a bun in the oven, whatever. And Bobby Mack was soon to be a father, whether he liked it or not.

As Erin was grimly contemplating her future, the bold Bobby was romancing the bikini bottoms off his latest squeeze – a forty-year-old cougar from Essex who had just engaged his services, and hopefully she'd get him to maintain the pool as well. Boy, was she something.

Thank God his mother wasn't home. He'd never get away with bringing a woman back to the house, and certainly not one as old as Dianne herself. But his father? Christ, he wouldn't notice if they were putting on a floor show in the middle of the lounge. He supposed it was time he got a place of his own. At his age, to still be living at home with Mummy and Daddy was definitely not cool. But hey, he liked it. He had all his home comforts, his laundry was taken care of, his food provided, all for free. And he actually liked his parents and how they lived. The only disadvantage was the lack of privacy, but seriously, was it worth giving all this up? What were hotel rooms for?

Now he knew why his ma had taken off back to Scotland. Old Frankie boy was back on the scene. And boy, did his mother hate the old priest with a vengeance. There had been one helluva ding-dong after the last visit and Dianne had vowed she would personally turf both of them out on their arses if the priest darkened their door again. But Daddio was having none of it and she'd obviously been shipped out. It looked like he'd won that battle. But would he win the war? That remained to be seen.

Bobby didn't mind the old boy, in fact he found him quite droll. Oh, he wouldn't trust him as far as he could throw him, and he was never sure if the old bastard had tried it on with him years ago when Bobby was very young. He did remember his mother going for Frank with a huge metal frying pan, so maybe he had. Whatever. It was a long time ago and he'd never tried anything since, so maybe Bobby had just got the wrong end of the stick.

He did, however, puzzle over the years what the connection was between Pete and the priest. Hey, Bobby wasn't daft and he had lived in Marbella amongst the criminal fraternity long enough to know that the pair were up to no good, but so what? He had no idea and, quite frankly, even less interest. Let them get on with it, whatever it was. They'd been at it for years and no breath of scandal had ever circulated. Whatever *it* was, *it* certainly provided a very nice lifestyle, thank you very much.

Those two had been closeted in the office for a couple of hours and from the sound of the raised voices, it didn't seem to be going his father's way. Pete Mack was the most genial of men when things were going well, but when they weren't? Shit, he was not a nice person to be around. Anyway, time to dump the old chick and meet up with the boys. Every night was party night in Bobby's world.

Talk about bad luck, Marie Coyle hadn't been on holiday for God knows how many years, but had let herself be talked into going away for a couple of weeks by the latest man in her life. Having persuaded her brother to let Erin loose, she could hardly use the same argument herself.

So, just when Erin desperately needed her, Marie was sipping cocktails aboard the *Adventure of the Seas*, setting sail from Miami, totally unconcerned about her brothers, mother and sister-in-law, or business. Someone else could take care of the lap dancers and their problems and the masseurs with theirs. She'd either be missed and more thought of, or nobody would realise she'd gone and she'd have to look for something else. Whatever, she didn't give a damn right now. The only passing concern she had was for Erin. Whatever was wrong with the girl, it couldn't be that drastic and she'd fix it when she got back.

He was a fly old bugger, mused Pete Mack, never around when a shipment was in transit. The most dangerous time, the time when anything could go wrong, but due to Pete's exact planning and use of only the most professional forgers and couriers, it meant that up until now things had always gone as planned.

The police reckoned the first 48 hours in any missing person case were critical and Pete agreed wholeheartedly. He always insisted on having the merchandise out of the country of origin and well under way within half that time. He knew that once the alarm had been raised, all ports and airports were off limits, but with the new technology available, even that was cutting it fine. At the touch of a button, information, which would have taken days, or maybe even weeks to filter through, was available almost immediately and for the first time, two of his couriers had been detained. It had been a heart stopping situation, but fortunately for them, all the passports and documentation were first class.

For years there had been a bone of contention between the two partners. Frank wanted to cut back, to pay less for the services, and Pete had always refused. They used Reg Galloway, one of the best forgers around, but also one of the most expensive. Reg was old school and the fact that he had never had as much as a pull, stood testament to his work. It was certainly up to standard, enough to fool the Spanish authorities. But that one incident had forced Pete to come to a decision, one he had been mulling over since he'd taken over the Princess, and one that Canon Francis (he could never get used to calling him Frank) was not going to like.

It was time to call it a day; he'd had enough, he wanted out, and he was finished. They'd had a good run for their money and the rewards had been phenomenal. But now, with the influx of Russian and Eastern Europeans entering the market, the price had come down considerably and rendered the huge risks hardly worth it. So, against Dianne's wishes, he had invited his business partner over to Spain for what would hopefully be his last visit.

As usual, the wily old coot was pleading poverty. That might work with anyone else, but Pete was well aware of how much money had been paid to him over the past ten years and it ran into hundreds of thousands. Their game had been so specialised and extremely lucrative that up until recently they could name their price. O'Farrell had to have stashed away enough to singlehandedy support the IRA. And if he hadn't, it wasn't Pete's concern.

Over the years Pete had built up a reasonable portfolio of legitimate businesses, and with the recently acquired Marbella Princess, (he'd made the previous owner an offer he couldn't refuse), there was more than enough to support his lifestyle. He didn't need the hassle or the exposure to danger that his procurement business involved.

Dianne

"I'm telling you, Pete, forget it. He's been here twice this year already and I'm not skivvying after that old pervert again. I told you the last time, it's him or me, so make up your mind," Dianne screamed at him across the dining room table.

"Okay, no contest, sweetheart. Go pack your bags." Pete wiped the smirk right off her Botoxed face.

It had always suited him to let folk think Dianne wore the trousers in their relationship. This was definitely not the case, and nobody, especially not her, would tell Pete Mack what to do. This ultimatum had been a long time brewing.

"You can fuck right off, Mr Big Shot. The only one packing their bags here is you. Do you really think you can get rid of me that easy? Hey, I don't think so."

"Look, Dianne, be reasonable. This is the last time, I promise. He and I have done a fair bit of business together over the years, that's why he's had to stay as our guest. But now that I'm closing the operation down, there will be no reason for him to visit. So be a good girl, shut your mouth, and soon he'll be history, one way or another."

"Don't you tell me to shut up, you wanker. Maybe I should start shouting my mouth off? Letting folks know what you two have really been getting up to, eh? What do you say to that, fuckwit?"

"Don't push your luck, you've no idea what you're talking about."

"Is that so, smart-arse? Do you really think I've not sussed out what the two of you have been importing and exporting since the get go? A bit of business? Believe me, I know enough, enough to send you and him on a very long holiday courtesy of Her Majesty."

"Shut the fuck up, you stupid mare, I don't know what you *think* you know, but supplying a little bit of gear to pay the grocery bills isn't going to put me away or him for that matter."

"A bit of gear, you are fucking joking. Let's put it this way, you've always hated kids and how we managed to ever conceive Bobby is a miracle in itself. But since we came here and you teamed up with that dirty shagging priest you suddenly became the 'Pied Piper'. Oh I know exactly what you've been up to, so you make up your mind. I'll ask you again, him or me?"

Pete stormed off the terrace, he had the greatest urge to put his hands round her scrawny throat and squeeze hard. He needed time to think, there was no way she was calling the shots, no way. Calm down, he drilled himself. Calm down and think this through.

Did he want rid of Dianne? Of course he did but her disappearing just now would raise too many questions. Unfortunately, she was one of the leading lights in Marbella, and as the wife of the biggest club owner, she couldn't just vanish. The answer was to send her back home to Scotland. Her mother and sister now lived way out in the sticks, a far cry from the city where they'd all grown up. It was unlikely she'd run into anyone from the old days but it was a chance he'd have to take.

This should quieten her down for now, and give him the opportunity to sort out his other problem. Unlike Dianne, Frank's disappearance wouldn't cause a stir here. His random visits were unlikely to provoke any unwanted questions. Over in Glasgow, however, his disappearance would definitely cause quite an uproar, but thankfully there was nothing to connect him to Marbella. This was all hypothetical of course, his proverbial 'Plan B'. Maybe Frank would just accept that the goose that laid the golden eggs was dead, but he didn't think so.

Coincidence

"Come away in, Paddy, nice to see you." Father Jack had been expecting his visitor and had had the housekeeper make up a tray for the two men.

"Okay Mrs Gavin, that'll be all, thanks. We can do for ourselves." The priest ushered the reluctant house keeper out of the sitting room.

"She'll be desperate to report to himself what your visit is all about," chuckled the priest.

"Watch this." As he threw the door wide, the miserable-faced old woman almost fell headlong into the room. "Was there something else, Mrs Gavin?"

"No Father, I was just . . ."

The ringing of the telephone saved the housekeeper from further embarrassment.

"I'll just get that, will I, Father?"

"Yes, you do that and I don't want to be disturbed for the next hour." The priest retreated into the room, closing the door firmly behind him.

The two men sat down opposite each other still grinning at the nerve of the woman.

"Will I be mother?" smiled Father Jack, handing the delicate china cup and saucer to the big burly man.

By God, they do well by themselves, thought Paddy. "So, Father, what can I do for you?"

"I've a bit of a dilemma and I have to say I'm not sure what I should do, or where to start."

"I've always found the beginning is the best place," laughed Paddy. He was quite chuffed that the priest, for whatever reason, trusted him enough to ask for his help.

"The trouble is, I wasn't here at the beginning. But we'll give it a go anyway. I'm damned sure you know that this church has been the stomping ground for practically every IRA fugitive at one time or another, since the 'Troubles' began, and all courtesy of Canon Francis O'Farrell."

Paddy gave a derisory snort at the mention of his name. "Aye, it's the worst kept secret and has been for years," said Paddy.

"It has, son, yes it has, and as we're nearly all sympathisers, rightly or wrongly, we have tended to turn a blind eye," the priest went on. "Aye, and would probably have continued to do so."

"What's changed then? Have the authorities got wind of your would-be students? "

"Och, I'm damned sure they've always known, but it suited them to ignore the situation. No, it's closer to hand and far more serious, and as I said, I don't know what to do."

"Well, it would help if we *both* knew what the problem is."

"That's all very well, but once this is out there's no going back, Paddy, and I'm not sure who'll survive the fallout, but I can't just ignore it. The drugs were different."

"Drugs, what drugs?" Paddy was all ears.

"The drugs being dealt from within this parish by our illustrious guests."

"What? Are you trying to telling me that drugs are being dealt from here? This church, bang in the middle of my turf, across the street from my mother and I don't know about it?"

"Paddy, it's being going on since God knows when."

The big man was on his feet, pacing back and forth across the small sitting room, muttering under his breath.

"Right. I want to know the lot, every last ounce of information."

"Well, that's what you should be telling me, my boy, because according to my sources they claim to be working for the Coyles."

"I don't fucking believe this. You're telling me that these fuckers are dealing right under my nose?"

"Look, Paddy, you can sort the dealing later, that's not the reason I need help."

"Fuck, there's more?" spluttered Paddy. "Don't tell me, the nuns are turning tricks in the confessionals?"

"Paddy, remember who you're speaking to. I knew this was a bad idea," said Father Jack rising to indicate the meeting was finished.

"Oh no, you don't get away that easy. I want to

know the real reason for this little chat. What exactly has been going on? You may as well tell me, 'cause there'll be fucking ructions over this lot anyway."

"Maybe we should leave it for now? You've no idea how terrible the repercussions could be. I'm not even sure we can handle it ourselves."

"Father, I'm not leaving till you come clean and if it's that sensitive, you won't want my boys blundering through the chapel looking for Martin McGuiness and his cronies, because that's what's about to happen."

"Seriously, I don't know how to start, or even if I'm right. What if I've got the wrong end of the stick, what then? I'll have opened a massive can of worms for no reason."

"Look, sit down and tell me," an exasperated Paddy plonked the man in an armchair and sat down opposite.

"Now, begin. What happened first?"

"A phone call," answered the priest.

"Okay, you got a call or made a call?" This was going to be a long interview if he had to drag every sentence out of the old fella.

"I got a call, but it wasn't meant for me."

"Who was it meant for?"

The fact that there were only officially three residents meant there was a limited choice of recipients.

"Well, the caller was foreign and I couldn't understand a word he was saying."

"And?"

"I hung up. I thought it was a wrong number."

"And?"

"Well, Frank, Canon O'Farrell . . ."

"I know who Frank is. For the love of God, man, get on with it."

"Well, Frank came dashing in, in a hell of a stew, wanting to know who had phoned and what had been said. I told him it was a foreigner and was likely a wrong number, but he was so agitated. I've never seen him like that."

"And?"

"Well, at the time I thought it odd, but nothing more than that. He was like a cat on a hot tin roof. Every time the phone rang he bolted for it. To be honest, I found it extremely entertaining and I made a point of getting in his way, or picking it up before he could get to it. This went on for most of the day. As I said, I thought it was odd, but nothing sinister and I certainly never expected what I discovered."

"A couple of days later I walked into the study to find him on the phone. He was extremely irate with the caller and was insisting that under no circumstances was the person to call him at this number again, it was too dangerous. As soon as he realised he wasn't alone, he hung up and drivelled some rubbish about wrong numbers. Why would anyone threaten a wrong number? He was definitely threatening somebody and I assumed it was something to do with his house guests."

"He never gave any explanation?"

"Explanation, Frank? Absolutely not. He's above explaining himself, even God gets short shrift from our canon. "To be perfectly honest, whatever it was, I didn't want involved, let them all get on with it. It was two or three weeks after, in fact our man had just left for Spain, when I took another call from the mysterious wrong number. I almost missed picking it up and the answer machine had kicked in and actually recorded the conversation."

"Yeah?"

"It took a bit of time to understand what the call was all about and the guy on the other end obviously thought I was Frank."

"Have you still got the recording?"

"Yes, I changed the cassette right away, just as a little insurance premium."

"So what was so terrifying about this phone call?" queried Paddy.

"At first, nothing in particular. I thought it was something to do with an adoption which had somehow gone wrong. I was quite intrigued," said the priest.

"Aye, he always made a big thing about his involvement with the kids. I think he was expecting an OBE or something," smiled Paddy. "As if. Personally, I wouldn't trust the bugger as far as I could throw him."

"You're not the only one who feels like that about him, trust me. Anyway, I listened to the recording a few times, but still didn't understand what it was about. I knew there was something fishy going on."

"I decided to do a little detective work. It was perfect timing, with his lordship off on one of his jaunts, Mrs Gavin away in Ireland and no house guests. For the first time in heaven knows how long, I was actually in the house on my own, with just the daily woman for company and she'd left for the day."

"No room in a chapel house should be locked, there's nothing to hide, but the influx of house guests from across the water, many with somewhat shady backgrounds was excuse enough for Frank to keep his rooms locked and he had the damned keys with him."

"I'm no burglar, but, come hell or high water, I was determined to get in and have a look around. I thought there had to be a spare key somewhere in this mausoleum. Well, someone up there was looking after me. I remembered seeing keys in a box in the safe and lo and behold, didn't I strike lucky?"

"Don't tell me you found his stack of porn under the bed?"

"If only."

The Hunt

The men had been closeted for over two hours. Father Jack was completely exhausted at the end of the session, but by God, his opinion of the big man opposite him had changed dramatically. To be truthful, he had always regarded Paddy as nothing more than a big lump – an uneducated thug with a bit of veneer, having got to where he was by dint of his wife's money and her connections. The priest had never really given him credit for having the nous to stay at the top once he'd reached there.

This man was no lout, no brainless heavy. He was an astute businessman who could sum up a situation immediately, but who could also take a man out just as quickly. He was very dangerous and Father Jack knew he'd rather be on his side than against him. He would be thankful till the end of his days that Paddy Coyle regarded him as a friend and not an enemy.

"So what did you find, D.I. Taggart? Had there 'been a murder'?" Paddy goaded his companion.

"Several, as it happens," replied Father Jack.

"Go on, man, you're having a laugh, aren't you?"

"Believe me, I wish I was."

Father Jack, having gained access to his superior's accommodation, had no real idea what he was looking for, but his gut feeling was that there must be a reason for the canon taking such measures to keep intruders out. What was he hiding? This was probably the only chance he would have to find out.

In comparison to the rest of the house, these rooms were extremely well furnished. An expensive and comfortable Chesterfield, a couple of rugs which looked handwoven, and the television was a far cry from the old black and white thing he was forced to endure, but it was what was sitting in the corner that took his breath away: a sophisticated, high-tech, up to the minute computer.

Father Jack would have staked this week's collection that Canon Francis O'Farrell knew nothing about the world of computers, and if this was the case, what the hell was going on? Heaven above, Jack himself had no idea how to even turn it on. Well, that answered in part why the locked doors, but hey, there was more to this, of that he was absolutely sure.

"I turned the place upside down, Paddy, but there wasn't as much as a scrap of paper anywhere, not even the Catholic Times."

"What would he want with a computer?" Paddy himself had only just become familiar with the technology and he found it absurd that an elderly priest should be so up-to-date.

"Not 'just' a computer, Paddy. You should see this, it wouldn't look out of place in NASA."

"A bit over the top for writing his sermons, don't you think?"

"I do, but it gets even stranger."

There had to be more than a fancy suite and an up-to-date personal computer, but what? The rooms were almost clinical, with very few personal items, considering they had been occupied by the same man for twenty-odd years.

Exasperated and confused, Father Jack made one last sweep. He pulled out drawers, checked the bottoms of all the furniture and just as he was about to give up, bingo! He came across a key taped to the underside of the computer station.

"A key?" ventured Paddy. "What? A door key, a car key?"

"Neither," said the priest. "A fairly ordinary key like you would have for a money box, but it had what I thought was a serial number etched on to the barrel – AI 23 something – I can't remember offhand."

"I think I know what type of key you found."

"Well, it took me a while to work it out. But then, I don't live in a world of criminality or subterfuge."

"When did all this happen, by the way?" Paddy was intrigued by the priest's tale.

"Four days ago. I couldn't do anything over the weekend, so it was yesterday before I had a chance to do any checking."

"And?" prompted Paddy.

"Well, I was sure it was the Allied Irish Bank, given that we've had a stream of paddies, sorry, my boy, I wasn't thinking. Since we have played host to countless Irish men over the years. But I had no idea how I would get access to a safety deposit box. What would I need in the form of identification? O'Farrell had his passport with him and he'd never learned to drive so I was a bit limited."

"So what did you do?"

"Well, I bargained that most of the staff would be either Irish or Catholic and if confronted with a priest I could blag my way in. I took correspondence from the parish and my passport, but I didn't need anything."

"Really?" said an astounded Paddy. "They just let you walk in and rummage about in a safety deposit box?"

"Being a member of the clergy does have its advantages. That and the fact wee Linda Ryrie from Admiralty Street was on the desk, and the fact I baptised her, gave her first Holy Communion and took her confession on a Saturday helped."

"She escorted me through to the strongroom.

Apparently the possession of a key was all I required."

"Hey, on the next bank job I'll just take you and leave the shooter at home," joked Paddy. "Well, what was in it? A signed photo of Pope John Paul the Second and Mother Teresa in a compromising situation?"

"Paddy, please."

"Okay, Father, but can you get to the point?"

"Christ, laddie, I've not even scratched the surface. There was money, more money than I've ever seen in my life. More money than I could count and in different currencies, dollars, euros and sterling."

"It could be an IRA stash, nothing unusual in that." Paddy answered quickly.

"You could be right, but it wasn't only the money, there were documents – birth and death certificates."

"Again, it could be Irish connections."

"There were account books, lists, information on some kind of merchandise, payments and delivery dates. I don't think it was drugs, but it was the photographs of the children that got me. God knows how many of them, but they were strange. Don't ask me why, I don't know, but these snapshots were weird, certainly not what you'd expect a priest to keep hidden. I can tell you that there's something very wrong going on and I don't know what to do."

"What about his connections with the Adoption Society? That could account for them."

"Believe me, these were no photographs of poor little orphans, they were disturbing and, honest to God, I can't get them out of my head."

"Porn? Were they explicit?"

"No, but you know, it was like they were teasing or tantalising. Maybe that's why they seemed strange to me."

"Our illustrious canon is definitely up to no good, but you said murders. Don't tell me he had photographs of the dead bodies too?"

"No, but believe it or not, he had a little black book with names, dates and places."

"Get away. How do you know it was a record of murders?"

"Names crossed out and deceased written across them is a fairly substantial clue, a dead giveaway, wouldn't you say?"

"For fuck's sake, this is getting dafter by the minute."

"Oh, and I nearly forgot, there was another key, not the same as the first, but it looked like it was for a locker of some kind."

"A locker? What did you do with it? I'd like a look."

Father Jack crossed the room and from beneath the old black and white portable television he produced the key.

"There was no chance of it being found by the housekeeper, the lazy old beggar seldom dusts and certainly wouldn't shift anything."

"You're right. I'm sure this key is for a station locker. We use them from time to time." Paddy examined the key.

"The safest ones are at either Central or Queen Street Stations, so we should try them first."

"Today?" Father Jack queried.

"No, next Thursday . . . of course today. When is your man due back?"

"He's usually away for a week to ten days, but this trip wasn't scheduled so he could be longer or back tonight. I've no idea. And he certainly doesn't confide in me."

"Right, let's go, the car's outside."

Friendship

"I'm sorry, madam, but the store is closing in five minutes, I have to ask you to leave." The shop assistant knocking on the cubicle door was becoming quite agitated; trust her to get stuck with a nutter who'd locked herself in the bogs. She was hoping the guy from Accounts was going to be waiting for her at the staff entrance, but if she didn't get rid of this headcase soon, he'd be off.

"I'm going to have to call security, madam. The store is now closed, I need you to vacate the ladies room and make your way to the exit." Still nothing. Maybe it was a druggie, or a shop lifter? Oh God, they could turn violent if they got cornered. You heard of these situations all the time, especially here in Glasgow.

"Is there something wrong, madam?"

Still no reply. Shit, whoever it was could be unconscious or even dead. God, she hoped not. If that was the case she'd still be here at opening time tomorrow.

There was movement. Suddenly the door shot open and a young girl of maybe eighteen or nineteen dashed out. The first thing the assistant spotted was the test box and she could see that the girl had been crying. Shit, she'd been there herself a couple of times. Bugger. The guy from Accounts would keep.

"Hold on, wait a second." She picked up the empty box and continued. "It looks like you've had a bit of bad news maybe?"

The young girl barely nodded.

Why the fuck was she getting involved? She should just let her go. Her friends were right, she was an interfering so-and-so and maybe she should keep her nose out of other people's business. But she'd been desperate on a few occasions herself when she could have done with a kind word. She couldn't let this kid walk out on her own.

"Cat got your tongue?" she asked the youngster. "I'm Carol, what's your name, sweetheart?" Talking nineteen to the dozen she led the girl towards the exit, grabbing her bag and coat as they left the store.

"I know it's overwhelming, but there are ways of dealing with these situations. Let's grab a coffee and see if we can sort this mess out." Carol, leading the way, was completely oblivious to the fact that the girl she'd taken under her wing had not yet uttered a word.

The coffee shop was packed with young shop workers. It was warm, noisy and comforting. Erin felt like she was in a dream. How had she got here? Who was this girl handing her a hot steaming cup of something?

"Right, it would help to know your name for starters," Carol chirped at her.

"God," thought Erin. She was one of those do-gooders who was going to be a bugger to shake off. In her rush to leave the house, she'd just grabbed her keys. No bag, so no communication.

"Okay, it doesn't matter, you can tell me when we know each other a bit better," said her new best friend. "Does the father know?"

Erin just shook her head.

"Is he still around?"

Again she shook her head.

"Do you want to keep it?"

Erin pulled her crucifix from under her sweater and showed it to Carol.

"Well, that answers that question. Do you know how far on you are?"

Counting out the weeks on her fingers they came to the conclusion that it was maybe twelve weeks.

"And you've just worked out how late you are? Phew! What about your family?" asked Carol. "Okay, okay, calm down. I'm just going through all the options."

Erin grabbed a napkin and gestured to Carol to give her a pen or something to write with.

"I can't speak," she wrote.

"Oh. My. God." bellowed Carol and the coffee shop went deathly quiet, most of the occupants turned to stare at the two girls.

Why did everybody assume she was deaf as soon

as they discovered she had no speech? "Don't shout, I can hear perfectly well. I just can't answer."

Carol grabbed the pen and paper and wrote, "Sorry, sorry, I didn't think."

"Why the devil are you writing?" laughed Erin for the first time in a long time.

"I don't know," sniggered the shop assistant. "Let's start again."

"Hello, my name is Carol, and you are?"

"Erin."

"Okay, nice to meet you, Erin. Things are a bit shitty at the moment, aren't they?" Carol asked the young girl.

"A bit," she wrote.

"Do you want to tell me about it? Sometimes it's easier with a stranger. I promise I won't judge and I'll keep it to myself."

"I think I'm pregnant," wrote Erin. "No. I'm sure I'm pregnant," sliding the two sticks discreetly out of her pocket and showing them to her new friend.

"Yep, I'd say you were too."

An hour later, Carol had most of the story. Her family's overprotection, the holiday to Marbella, meeting Bobby and then being dumped. It was pretty clear to Carol that Erin had definitely not gotten over this man and to find out she was pregnant was the proverbial straw that broke the camel's back.

"What are you planning on doing?" she asked Erin.

"God knows. I only just realised that I was in this state a couple of hours ago. I thought I had a bug or something. I really don't know what to do, but I can't tell my family, that's out of the question."

"Sure you wouldn't consider a termination?"

"I'd consider almost anything right now, but not that. It's a mortal sin."

"Sorry, but I deal with the here and now, not the maybe and the hereafter, but, each to their own. First things first. You have to tell him. You never know, maybe he'll do the right thing. Anyway, you've nothing to lose. Why don't you phone him, see how the land lies?"

"Phone him how? Neither of us is telepathic."

"Shit, I forgot. Sorry. Get someone to phone him for you. What about one of your mates, the ones you were on holiday with? At least they know him."

"I'm not telling any of them, that would be right up their street."

"Okay then, I could phone him." Oh shit, this was getting her in even deeper. Why could she never keep her mouth shut? Carol argued with herself.

"Would you? I'd be so grateful, but when?"

"Let's not rush into this," Carol reasoned. "We need to think out exactly what you want to tell him 'cause let's face it, if you got a shock he's going to get a bigger one."

"Then surely I would be better going back to Marbella and seeing him face to face?"

"I suppose so, but what if, and this is a strong possibility, he just doesn't want to know?"

"I don't know, I really don't know."

"Look, it's my day off tomorrow, why don't we meet up and sort something out properly?"

"Are you sure?" Erin wrote. "I don't really have anyone I could trust. They're all scared stiff of my dad and would go straight to him."

"I've got a bad feeling about this," said Carol. "But who exactly is your dad and why is everyone so afraid of him?"

"Maybe better you don't know."

"No, I don't think so. I need to know who I'm dealing with, so tell me."

"I'm Erin Coyle, Paddy Coyle's daughter."

"Fuck! I'm damned if I do and damned if I don't," groaned Carol.

"Look, I understand if you don't want to get involved, but thanks anyway. At the very least you've helped me get my head a bit clearer."

"Just meet me at St. Enoch's at, say, 10am, and we'll take it from there."

"10am tomorrow, are you sure?"

"Yes I'm sure, see you tomorrow. And chin up, things will work out so don't worry."

Oh, everything would work out okay, but maybe not as they hoped. The girls went their separate ways; one jumped into her brand new Mini and drove to a luxury home and the other climbed on board a number 44 bus to pick up her daughter from the childminder.

End of …

"I'm telling you it's too dangerous," Pete snapped at the old priest. "You've no idea how close to the wind we've sailed over the past year. Anyway, I've disposed of the last two couriers so there's no going back now."

"Disposed of?" queried his partner. "As in, got rid of?"

"Well, you don't think for a minute that I was going to let them wander round Europe with a P45 and a redundancy cheque, did you? Of course I disposed of them."

"But I told you, I've taken a contract. Money up front as usual and delivery at the end of the month."

"Well, you'll just have to refund the money and tell them to go elsewhere."

"I can't, we're already committed. There's no way out. You know what these people are like."

"It's over, Frank. No more. Surely you've got enough to retire to a nice little island and spend the rest of your days in the sun?"

"Retire? Do you really think these guys will let me retire, priest or no priest?"

"Maybe you should have thought about that before you got involved in human trafficking."

"Human trafficking? What're you talking about, man? As far as anyone can prove I arranged adoptions for childless couples. I had no part in any trafficking, human or otherwise, and there's not a shred of evidence to link me to anything of the sort."

"Then it's all the more reason to get out now, ya old goat. The Russians and the rest of the Eastern Europeans have killed the goose. There are no more golden eggs, and I for sure have no intention of spending as much as one night in a Spanish jail. So if you want one more trip, you are on your own."

"You forget how much I know, Pete, and also who I know."

"Are you threatening me, you stupid old fucker? I would hate to think so, and do you really think if I'm going down, you're not coming with me? Fuck off!"

"Of course I'm not threatening you," the priest backtracked quickly. "Just one more trip, and that's the end."

"It can't be done. I knew you'd try this, so to make sure it was finished, all the infrastructure has been shut down. It can't be done. There is no support documentation so no, no last trip."

"Pete, you don't know what you've done, I'm a dead man walking."

"Hmm, you were anyway," Pete muttered to himself. "Don't be so bloody dramatic, you must have known things were changing, the money for a start."

"I have to fulfil this contract one way or another."

"Well, I'm sorry, Canon O'Farrell, but you're on your own with this one. I'm out."

The Journey

Erin had hardly slept a wink, the same words going round and round in her head. Pregnant. Her pregnant! What the hell was she going to do? Realistically, the best thing she could do for everyone's sake would be to have a termination. But she couldn't, she wouldn't be able to live with herself. If she went ahead and had the baby – even that sounded weird to her, 'the baby' – what life would either of them have? Certainly nothing like the one she had at present. Would Bobby stand by her? Truthfully, she didn't think she had a cat in hell's chance. But, he was the father and had a right to know.

What about the shop assistant, Carol? She was certainly very kind and appeared to want to help, but Erin didn't really hold out much hope that she'd turn up. Although she did seem very positive and capable, the sort you'd want on your team if you were in any kind of trouble. Whether she'd have second thoughts about getting mixed up with the Coyles remained to be seen. There was no question Erin would definitely be at St. Enoch at 10 am, but, if as she suspected, Carol was a no-show, she would go straight to the travel agents and book a trip. What would she tell her mum and dad? Where could she say she was off to without making them suspicious?

When she came down for breakfast, both Bridget and Paddy thought she looked even more washed out, probably due to the lack of sleep. The smell of her father's full Scottish breakfast hit the gag reflex and she had to dash from the table. The sounds of her vomiting could be clearly heard by both.

"You need to get that lassie back to the doctors and pronto," Paddy barked at his wife. She said nothing, but had he been more observant, Paddy would have noticed the pained look on Bridget's face. She was damned sure she knew exactly what was up with his precious daughter, and God help them all when it came home to roost.

"Sorry folks," the young girl apologised. "Hope I didn't put you off your breakfast." She pinched a sausage off her dad's plate just as she always did.

At nine fifty-five Erin parked her car and set off to meet her new friend.

"Hi, how are you?"

"Oh, okay, and who is this little person?" Erin tickled the little girl under her chin.

"This is Amy. Say hello to Erin, she's our new friend."

"Hello, Erin," mimicked the child.

Erin smiled and patted Amy on the head.

"If you're really good this morning we'll take you to the ball-pit in the centre." This was a firm favourite with mother and daughter, mainly because it was free.

"I'll be good, cross my heart, I'll be a good girl," she replied, jumping up and down with excitement.

As they crossed the square and entered the shopping centre, the two new friends chatted away. Well, one chatted and the other listened intently.

The ball-pit was busy, but Amy was off and running. This would give the two of them at least half an hour undisturbed peace to chat.

"I take it you haven't changed your mind about a termination?" Carol asked.

"No, I can't do it," Erin wrote. "I'm sorry, I know it's the easiest way out, but not for me, this is bad enough."

"Okay, I had to ask. Don't apologise. As you can see, it wasn't an option for me either."

"Are you on your own with Amy?" Erin asked, quite surprised. "How do you manage?"

"With great difficulty, let me tell you. It's hard work, make no mistake, and your life is never the same."

"But you get by?"

"Oh, I get by okay. Working for the minimum wage, a bit of jiggery pokery, a fake season ticket and living in a hellish bedsit. Yes, I get by, but it's not what I want for my child. Nor is it how I envisaged my life."

"But do you regret it?"

"Don't be bloody stupid, of course I regret it, and what would I do if I could turn the clock back? Well, I would be a fully qualified stylist and I wouldn't get pregnant, that's for sure, but it doesn't mean I would give her up. No, not for all the money in the world. Just don't think it's easy."

"I don't and I'm terrified. I don't think he'll want to know, but I have to try."

"Okay, let's decide what the best way forward is. What about family?"

"My auntie Marie would definitely help, but she's off in the Caribbean and won't be back for a couple of weeks, so she's no good. My granny Lizzie, well, she's already dealt with this before with Marie and Errol, but somehow it would be different for me."

"What about your mum? Surely she'd stand by you?"

"She'd do exactly what my dad told her to do."

"Well, what about your dad then?"

"Nope."

"Are you sure? You seem like a close family. Things happen in life and that's when the family comes together. I just think there's more to this, and I hope that it's the baby you're putting first, and you're not just using it to get him back, 'cause trust me, that won't work. If Bobby had any real feelings for you, he would never have let you leave at the end of the holiday. You wouldn't be sitting here wondering what his reaction is going to be. I know this is harsh, but you have to face facts. Chances are, he'll be on his toes as soon as he sees you, and then where will you be?"

Carol, having spent nearly all her early years in the care system, knew only too well how easily kids were dumped, but hey, Erin wasn't a kid − she was eighteen and should be able to fend for herself. But Carol knew full well this young girl would be lucky to last a couple of weeks on her own, so they had to have a plan.

"Should we phone him?" Erin asked.

"I'm worried that if we do that, it's a case of forewarned is forearmed," said Carol.

"Why?"

"Well, what reason would you have to contact him? It wouldn't take a genius to put two and two together and he'd be up and away before the dialling tone ended."

"That wouldn't surprise me. So what do you suggest?"

"Under normal circumstances, I'd say jump on the next flight and go back to face him. But that's not so easy for you."

"For Christ's sake, Carol, I've got all my faculties bar one, and it's no different than getting on a bus. I'll show the driver my ticket. Look, I'm not retarded. I can travel on my own."

"Hey, calm down. Remember, I'm on your side. My worry is the language, what if something happens? You have difficulty in communicating here, so it's going to be twice as hard in another country."

"It's Spain, most people speak English," wrote Erin.

"Yeah, if it's two beers, but not, 'Please can you take me to the hospital, my baby's coming early.' You need someone to travel with you, Erin. What about one of the girls you went on holiday with? Surely one of them could be trusted?"

"No, it would get round like wildfire."

"Look, if you're going to get hell from your parents, why not just front it out now and get it over and done with? I think you might be surprised. I can't see them throwing you out to fend for yourself. It's 1994, no big deal."

"Listen, where I'm concerned it's 1894, and always will be."

"Okay, then who are we going to get to go with you?"

"You could come with me."

"Don't be daft. First of all, I've got Amy to think about. Secondly, I'll get the sack, and anyway, I couldn't afford to go to Saltcoats never mind Spain. And I don't have a passport, so that rules me out."

"Number one, we take Amy with us. Two, I'll pay for us all. Three, so what if you get the sack − I'll get you a better job with the family and Portcullis House is just round the corner so we could have your passports by lunchtime."

"Look Erin, you don't know me, I could be anything − a serial killer, a con-artist, anything."

"Christ, Carol, you're dealing with a Coyle. Any of those would be a normal day at the office."

At that precise moment a flushed, excited little girl came running over to her mum and her mum's friend.

"I'm fursty mummy, I need a drink."

"Just think, a few days in the sun would do her the world of good."

"There must be someone else who could go."

"Nope, or at least no-one I could trust. Say you'll come, please Carol, please?"

By the end of the day the passports had been acquired, flights to Alicante had been booked, together with a family room at the Marbella Riu, a very smart four star hotel, right in the centre of the resort and only five minutes' walk from the Marbella Princess nightclub, Bobby Mack's favourite night spot.

What to tell the parents was the next hurdle. She'd come up with something, the trick was to make it simple.

Evidence

First stop, the Allied Irish bank. The two men walked up to the customer service desk to be greeted by the same youngster Father Jack had dealt with on his previous visit.

"Back again, Father? Oh hello, Mr Coyle, how's Erin? I've not seen her for ages," chatted Linda.

"She's fine, just started her first year at university, studying law."

"Good, tell her I'm asking after her. Can I get either of you gentlemen anything? Tea, coffee?"

"No, we're fine Linda. I'll ring the bell when we're ready to go." Father Jack turned and motioned to Paddy to sit down.

"Jesus wept," said Paddy "between the cash and the bearer bonds, there's enough here to buy a small country."

"I didn't even know what they were," Father Jack replied stacking the bonds on the table. "Each one is worth fifty thousand."

A quick glance at the ledgers and documents was enough for Paddy. The photographs were as the priest had described and Paddy sussed right away what the old fucker had been involved in. Adoption my arse, he thought. But what to do next?

"Look, Father, if we leave this here the bastard could come back, empty the lot and be away on his toes. And where is our proof then?"

"But he's going to miss it at some point."

"So? He can hardly go to the police and report three quarters of a million in bearer bonds, cash and a whole load of dodgy holiday snaps missing, can he?"

"True, but what'll we do with all this? What if we get caught with it?"

"Well, what do you want to happen? Surely you don't think he can come back and continue his life as a priest, tending to the sick and needy? Christ, he's looking at twenty years minimum, and that's not counting the poor fuckers that are holding up the flyovers on the M8."

"God Almighty, it's a hundred times worse than I thought. What are we going to do, Paddy?"

"First of all, we are going to empty this lot and hand the key back to that wee lassie and get ourselves right out of here, pronto."

Always prepared, Paddy produced a black holdall and within minutes had packed the contents of the box. Signing for the return of the key, they headed back to the car.

Their next call was to Queen Street station, round to the left luggage area. No luck, the key to number

83 was firmly in place. They made a quick trip to Central Station where they struck lucky.

Donning a pair of leather gloves Paddy discreetly opened the bag jammed in the narrow space.

"Fuck!" exclaimed the big man.

"What's wrong? What's in it?" the priest asked, craning to view the contents.

"Don't touch anything," Paddy commanded, pushing the priest aside.

"It's full of clothes, stained clothes, and going by the size, I would say they're young childrens' clothes."

Paddy stuffed everything back into the bag, closed the locker and hustled the priest quickly out on to the concourse to the waiting car.

"There are cameras all over the place in here, so put your head down and just keep walking," he instructed.

"But we've not done anything," said Father Jack indignantly.

"Try telling that to the judge when he asks if you know anything about a bag full of blood-stained kids' clothes, now keep going."

Back in the sanctity of Paddy's Jaguar, the priest looked on the verge of breaking down.

"Hey, chin up, Father, we'll get through this."

"What are we going to do, Paddy? This is big stuff for me."

"Fuck, you don't think this is big for me too?"

"Well, this is a lot more your style than mine. I can't stop thinking about the shame it's going to bring on my church."

"You know, I've hated that old bastard since I was twelve years old. He thrashed me and then my brothers. I vowed one day I'd pay him back. But I want you to believe me I never ever thought he would be involved in something like this."

"Nor I, my boy, nor I."

"My mother confesses her sins to him for fuck's sake!"

"Maybe he's just holding the keys for somebody? He might not be involved."

"C'mon, Father, would you risk the consequences for this little lot? Would you put yourself and St Jude's at risk for this kind of favour? No, I didn't think so. That's what we have to remember. He *is* involved, he's not the Lone Ranger and it's very likely that Tonto and the rest of the Indians are going to come looking."

"Surely they won't come after us, we know too much?"

"That's all the more reason for them to shut us up. Don't you worry about that, I've got enough troops to guard the Vatican, just stay calm."

The two men drove on in silence, the priest praying like he'd never prayed before and Paddy busy formulating a plan to get them out of this mess and make sure those responsible got their just desserts.

Plan of Action

"First things first," said Paddy. "I need to get our Michael, he's the man for the computer, there's nothing our boy doesn't know about them."

"Can you trust him?"

"I can trust him a bloody sight more than you can trust your partner, Father. For fuck's sake, he's my brother. Of course I can trust him. Not that it would matter either way. We have to get access to that machine and I don't know anyone else who could do the job."

They pulled up outside his mother's house and the smell of cooking came wafting out. Lizzie almost fell over backwards seeing her eldest son with Father Jack, obviously the best of pals. "Come away in, Father, I've just made a batch of scones. You'll stay and have a cuppa?" she prattled on.

"Sorry, Lizzie, but we're in a bit of a rush, another time," said Father Jack, much to Lizzie's disappointment.

She was old school and a visit from the priest was either a great accolade or great trouble. She knew her boys wouldn't bring trouble to her door.

Michael was on his third scone, butter and homemade jam oozing out, making the priest's mouth water while his insides were going like the clappers and it was taking all his might to keep him from roaring out to them to get moving.

"It's Michael we're after," said Paddy to his mother.

"And what, pray, would our Michael be able to do for Father Jack? Him that's not been inside the church for God alone knows how long."

"He doesn't want him to be an altar boy, if that's what you're getting at, Ma." quipped Paddy.

"Now, you wouldn't want me to break someone's confidence, would you?" Father Jack addressed Lizzie.

"Are you ready?" Paddy asked as Michael wiped jam from the corner of his mouth.

"What about me?" piped up Sean, "Is my soul not worth saving?"

"Of course it is, but for a different reason," said Paddy to the two intrigued men.

The church was a few minutes walk from Lizzie's front door, but all four piled into the Jaguar and drove the short distance to shield them from prying eyes. Too late, the jungle drums were already beating.

"We'll need to get rid of Mrs Gavin, Father. Can you send her on an errand or something?"

"God, she'd never take orders from me," said the surprised priest.

"Well, you'll have to get rid of her somehow. We can't have her hovering about."

"Oh, you're back, Father, and with visitors too," said the smarmy housekeeper. Will you be wanting something to eat? Maybe a late lunch or early afternoon tea?" she asked in the broadest of Irish brogues.

"Not at the moment, Mrs Gavin, but the bishop will be calling at around four. Could you rustle up something then? There'll be us four, himself and his assistant."

"Father Jack, you can't spring functions like this on me at such short notice."

"Will I be telling him he must have a fish supper from across the road, or that St. Jude's housekeeper can't provide him with a bite to eat? Imagine what the other housekeepers would make of that, you'd never raise your head again. Away with you, woman!" Father Jack handed her a twenty pound note and chased her off to the shops.

"If things weren't so serious I'd be dancing round the room. That's the first time she's every taken any kind of order from me," he said.

"Well, forget her for the moment, let's get on. Where's the key, Father?"

Unlocking the door, the four men entered Canon O'Farrell's inner sanctum. It was obvious the twins were surprised at the quality of the furnishings.

"It looks like a five star hotel," said Sean.

"Aye, and with all the mod cons. That computer cost a few bob," from Michael.

"That's where we need your help. We need to know for definite what the old bugger's been up to and I'm pretty damned sure it's all in there." Paddy was still somewhat distrustful of the technology, but his brothers, both of them, were a different generation altogether.

"Okay," said Michael switching the computer on. With a gentle hum the screen lit up. "Most folks have a password to keep others out of their business. I'm assuming the canon has one too. Yes, it's asking for one. Now, most people use one which is familiar and easy to remember. Let's try his date of birth. No, it's not that. Let's try . . ." and he began typing, "St. Jude's, no, it's not that."

"What about his mother's maiden name? Can you think of anything significant, Father Jack?"

"The only thing I've ever known him to talk about was the dog he had when he was a lad."

"Okay, what was the dog's name?" asked Michael.

"Rebel, as much for the cause as for the dog," answered Father Jack.

"Bingo!" exclaimed Michael as the screen sprang to life.

There were hundreds of ambiguous emails, but without knowing exactly what the merchandise was that was referred to, there was little incriminating evidence. Michael trawled through hundreds of sites, checking the computer's history which was bizarre, to say the least.

It was beginning to seem unlikely that Michael would find any answers when Paddy, fascinated by the unlikely sites that the man had visited, posed the question.

"Could there be a link between these sites that he's been visiting? There has to be something, you can't imagine him in here sitting at a screen looking at chemists, shoe shops, interior designers and so on. So there has to be something."

"Wait a minute," exclaimed Michael, clicking on a symbol at the bottom of the screen.

"Fuck sake," from Sean.

"Oh my God, what have we opened up?" cried Father Jack.

Paddy Coyle said nothing. He had suspected all along what Canon O'Farrell seemed to be heavily involved in, but to actually see images on a screen were more than Paddy could stomach. Page after page of the most depraved, horrendous, sickening images filled the screen and also the minds of the four men in the room.

Canon O'Farrell had just signed his own death warrant.

The Housekeeper

The bishop calling round for a bite to eat, how stupid did they think she was? In the twenty years she had been housekeeper at St. Jude's, the bishop had never 'just called round'. Nor was he ever likely to, especially when the senior clergyman was not in residence. So what the devil was going on and why was Father Jack as thick as thieves with those rag tags, the Coyle brothers?

From the vantage point of her scullery Imelda Gavin could observe most of the goings-on in the house, and right now, through the back window, she could see the four men in what should be a locked room, gathered around her brother's computer. And from the expressions on their faces, it looked serious.

She'd come to work in St. Jude's not long after her younger brother Francis, the newly appointed parish priest, had taken up residence. She, having recently been widowed, her husband the victim of a bombing raid that had gone wrong, was now a martyr to 'The Cause'.

She was a vicious and vindictive woman who cared only for the fight for freedom, as it was known, and her brothers. She would gladly give her life for any of them. Few, if any, knew that Mrs Gavin and Canon O'Farrell were even related, much less brother and sister and both did everything to maintain the status quo. It more than suited their purposes for both parishioners and the hierarchy to believe that they merely came from the same village, but that was where the connection ended.

Imelda cared not a jot for anyone's opinion of her and any deed, no matter how dreadful, was acceptable if it served her beloved Ireland. Over the years, to lighten her brother's load, she had taken on the responsibilities for the movement and safekeeping of what they called the soldiers of war. What had to be done was done with no remorse or guilt and it was she who had first persuaded her brother to become involved with Pete McClelland to expand his 'Procurement Business', never envisaging the sums of money involved.

The men had been closeted in the canon's room for the best part of an hour and she could contain herself no longer as she marched through the house and into the bedroom.

"I don't think Canon O'Farrell would be happy at strangers being in his private quarters." she addressed the priest.

"Oh, he'll be fine once he sees what Mr Coyle here plans to do with the place."

"I would be happier if you waited till the canon returns." Mrs Gavin stared pointedly at Father Jack.

"And why on earth would we be interested in whether you are happy or not? And what reason would there be to wait until the canon's return, which by the way could be weeks away?" replied Father Jack.

"He'll be home by the weekend," the housekeeper retorted.

"Good, that gives us another few days to finalise things." Father Jack drew himself up to his full height. "Thank you, Mrs Gavin, that will be all. You can go now."

"I need to lock up after you gentlemen, just to make sure."

"To make sure of what? No, you're fine. We're not quite finished with the measuring and since it's only you and I in residence, I don't think we need to worry." He closed the door with a bang.

"You can bet your life she'll be on to him toute suite and he'll be on the next plane, so we have to work fast," said Michael.

Imelda Gavin was beside herself with temper, marching back through the house to her kitchen and into the scullery where she was again able to spy on the four of them, still crowded round the computer. She had to contact Francis; he would know what these interfering low-lifes could have access to.

Thankfully she had insisted, many years ago, that he left her a number to contact him in an emergency. This was the first time she had ever been tempted. She would wait till Father Jack went off to take confession.

"Hello Villa Blanca."

"Hello, can I speak with Canon O'Farrell please?"

"Who's speaking?"

"Mrs Gavin, his housekeeper."

"I'm sorry, he's not in at the minute, do you want to leave a message?"

"Is that you, Pete?" queried the woman. Why would Pete McClelland pretend not to know her?

"Pete, it's Imelda. I have to get in touch with him, it's urgent. We have a problem back here."

"Sorry, my dear, I was just being extra cautious. He's not here just now, I think he went down to the Mission earlier, but I'm not sure. What's the problem?"

"I've had Father Jack and the Coyles snooping around for the best part of the day and they've been on his computer for most of that time. I'm worried Pete, really worried."

"Look, don't panic; I'll go find him and phone you back."

"As quick as you can. I'll be on my own until about eight, then Father Jack will be around."

The line went dead.

Pete was furious. The stupid old fool had given his number out to a bloody housekeeper, Christ, he might as well have announced their connection from the pulpit. Now he really would have to take action.

*

Sipping a large brandy in a discreet little bar in the old town, Frank was enjoying the company of a beautiful young Algerian boy called Ahmed whom he'd met yesterday. The lad was a bit older than Frank usually preferred, but at least at this age he could be seen in public and this little diversion would take his mind off his more pressing problems.

Pete had no difficulty locating his quarry. The old priest was a creature of habit and there were only two or three bars that Frank would frequent. Pete struck lucky in the third. His stomach flipped as he watched the old pervert caressing the young boy.

It really was time to sever the connection.

"My, my, to what do we owe the pleasure of your company?" drawled Frank, still caressing his young companion.

"Get rid of him, we have a problem," barked Pete.

"I don't think so. Remember, I'm on holiday."

"I said get rid. I've had the blessed Imelda looking for you. It seems your understudy has been entertaining visitors."

"Imelda looking for me?" the elderly priest paled. "Visitors, what visitors?"

"The Coyles. Now why would that bunch of arseholes be interested in your computer?"

"I don't know, but if she's worried so should we be."

Hurrying back up to the villa Canon O'Farrell was a worried man. "Why didn't you stop them?" he yelled at his sister.

"They were already in when I got back. Father Jack

had spun some ridiculous cock and bull tale about the bishop visiting."

"The bishop visiting? What the hell was he coming for?"

"He wasn't, it was simply a ruse to get rid of me."

"And you fell for it? You stupid fool."

"Of course I didn't, but they had a key to your room and there wasn't much I could do."

"Go into my room now and check under the computer table. See if there's a key taped there. Go now, I'll hang on."

The echo of footsteps could be heard as the house keeper let herself back into her brother's quarters.

"No, no key. And before you ask, I have checked thoroughly."

"Damn," swore the priest. "Damn. Okay, we'll have to move quickly. If they don't have the computer, they have no proof. I'll phone you back directly."

Coming off the phone, the canon was deep in thought.

"Well, what's it about?" asked Pete anxiously.

"I don't know how, but the Coyles have got wind of something. The key to the safety deposit box is missing, so we can safely assume they've cleared me out, but it's the computer I'm worried about. It's the most incriminating, because everything else can be attributed to The Cause, but not that. I need to get it disposed of now, I'm surprised they didn't take it, but trust me, they will."

"For fuck's sake, Frank. How could you be so stupid?"

"It's been working fine for years, this is just a little glitch. Get me Imelda back, will you? I know just how to take the wind out of Mr Coyle's sails."

"Imelda, it's me. We have to disable the computer ASAP, so you have to make sure that Father Jack is in a deep sleep. Put a couple of your sleeping pills in his hot chocolate, that will knock him out."

"Okay, what next?" queried Imelda.

"Wait for the knock. I'm sending a couple of lads to fix the problem."

"What if he doesn't want a drink?"

"For feck's sake, woman, stand over him till he drinks it."

"I take it they'll smash the thing up so no-one else can get into it?"

"Better than that, they'll simply take the main board out which will take minutes and the computer won't look as if anyone's been near it. Not, that is, until it's turned on and then nothing will happen. There will just be a blank screen. No memory, no problem."

"How the fuck do you know all this?" Pete had to admit he was impressed by Frank's knowledge, but it didn't change his opinion that once this disaster was sorted, he'd have to go, and not back to Blighty.

A boating accident, maybe?

The Return

"This is your captain speaking, welcome aboard Flight BA345 to Malaga. We are now cruising at 50,000ft and the outside temperature is minus 40 degrees. Our estimated time of arrival is 12.08."

Erin Coyle was an entirely different girl from the one who had first heard a similar announcement only weeks ago. Now there was no excitement about going off on her own, none of the silly chatter on her first flight. She still felt dread that somehow her father had found out and would storm the plane and drag her home. But no, not even the omnipotent Paddy Coyle could work that fast.

She had simply left a note on her pillow when she crept out of the house just before 6am.

'Gone away for a few days just to get my head cleared, don't worry, I'll be back soon.
Love Erin xx'

Bridget found it three hours later when she went to waken her daughter, thinking she'd overslept.

"Jesus, Mary, Mother of God."

What had the stupid fool done? An abortion clinic, that's where the silly girl had gone to. Would there be time to stop her? That was if she could trace the clinic, there were dozens throughout the city and how on earth would she keep it from her father?

While Bridget was poring through the Yellow Pages, Paddy was equally engrossed in the problems of the previous evening. It had been a big mistake to leave the computer in situ and as soon as he had his wits together he would rectify the situation. Where could he store it though? That was the problem. If he got caught with it, there was nothing to tie the contents to O'Farrell. Paddy couldn't think of him as his parish priest any longer, the man was an animal.

A quick cup of coffee, a slice of toast and he was out of the house and on his way. Was it his imagination, or was Bridget a bit off this morning? And no sign of his beloved daughter. God, they've obviously fallen out and he was thankful he wasn't to blame this time.

His journey into the city was uneventful but arriving at St. Jude's, he was met with by an extremely agitated Father Jack.

"Stop worrying, man, everything's under control. I'm going to take the computer from the premises for safekeeping. Listen, he'll probably know by now that we're on to him, so just keep calm and say nothing. I have to say, you look like shit."

"Trust me, I feel like it. I've got the hangover from hell and although not a drop passed my lips last night, I've got a mouth like the bottom of a bird's cage."

"You sure you didn't have a wee nightcap?"

"No, in fact I was about to pour myself one when her ladyship came in with a cup of hot chocolate. I was pleasantly surprised since, as you know, she'd gone off in a huff."

"Oh, for the love of Jesus. You *do* know what she did?" asked Paddy. "I should have sussed it and warned you."

"Sussed what? What did she do?"

"She spiked your drink, drugged you, probably with sleeping tablets. That's why you feel like shit. Have you checked the room? My guess is the bloody computer will be long gone."

When they opened up the room, to their surprise everything looked intact. The computer was exactly where they'd left it the day before. The men unplugged the machine and carried it out to Paddy's car.

"I'll be in touch later this morning, once I know how we are going to play this," with that, Paddy was off.

He had arranged to meet his brothers at one of the scrapyards, just in case he had to get rid of the evidence quickly and because they could work on the contents uninterrupted.

Sean and Michael were already waiting for him and neither looked best pleased.

"Morning, boys." Paddy gave them the heads up on what had happened at St. Jude's.

"What exactly are you planning to do with this stuff, Paddy?" asked Michael.

"Honestly, I don't know. We've got to find a way to shut him down and still keep it under wraps for Father Jack's sake."

"So you're not thinking of cashing in on it?" Sean questioned.

"For fuck's sake, man, what do you take me for, a nonce? Trust me, that old bastard will suffer just as much as each of those kids did, take my word for it."

"Sorry Paddy, we didn't think you would, but business is business."

"Not that kind of business. One thing that does concern me though, and needs to be sorted, is that that last lot of Micks who were staying in St Jude's appeared to have been dealing on our turf and in our name for fuck knows how long."

"Rubbish," said Sean. "There's nothing goes on that I don't get to know about."

"Well, this slipped under the wire, boy, and the only way it could, is through a doubler. At the least one of our guys is shifting their stuff and ours. Now, I want to know who and when I find out, God help them."

Meanwhile, Michael, engrossed in the set-up of the computer, seemed to be having some difficulty. "Sean, hand me that screwdriver, I can't get this fucking thing to open up. There's power and the lights are on, but nothing else."

"Maybe something got knocked loose in the move?" ventured Paddy. "But we were extra careful handling it."

Michael opened the casing and let out a curse. "Fucking bastards. You wouldn't fucking believe it."

"What's wrong?" shouted Paddy.

"What's wrong? I'll tell you what's fucking wrong. Some clever cunt has only come in and taken the guts out of this. All that's left is a shell. I never suspected a dickey bird. That's why the old witch drugged Father Jack, so he wouldn't hear anything or interrupt them. You have to hand it to O'Farrell, he's no mug."

"So what do we do now?" Sean said, kicking the door, "we can't touch him."

"Oh, I think we've hurt them alright, remember I've got the best part of three quarters of a million of his dosh and a key to a locker that would put him away for a nice long holiday."

"Aye, but if we get caught with the key, we do the time," a disgruntled Michael put forth.

"I'll deal with that, you two get on to the dealer's case and meet me back here later."

While all this activity was going on at home, Erin and her travelling companions were checking into their hotel right in the centre of Marbella. Carol was failing miserably at trying hard to be pleased and grateful. She felt awful and put it down to airsickness, but it was nearly two hours since they'd landed and she was still in a bad way.

"Look, I'll take Amy and go and get you something to settle your stomach. Have a lie down, we'll be back soon." Erin scribbled the note.

Carol was fast asleep in the darkened room before her friend and daughter got out of the lift.

Amy was as excited as a frisky puppy dancing along the seafront, past the cafes and bars full of glamorous holidaymakers. She was on the lookout for the green cross of the pharmacy to get something to make her mummy better.

"I see it, I see it," the little girl squealed, taking off like a shot. She ran in and out of the crowds, her eye on the green cross and ran slap bang into an elderly gentleman, out walking with his grandson.

"Whoa there, girlie, where are you going in such a rush?" said the nice old man in a sing-song Irish lilt.

Erin raced up to them and grabbed Amy by the arm, shaking her to let her know how angry she was. Turning to the man, Erin almost collapsed on the spot. Looking at him, dressed in baggy shorts and a lurid Hawaiian shirt, she thought it couldn't be. No way, but it was.

"Erin, what a surprise," said the elderly man. "Are you on holiday with the family?" terrified that Big Paddy Coyle would appear in front of him any minute.

Erin shook her head and wrote, "No, with friends, nice to see you, in a hurry," and off she ran into the pharmacy. With some difficulty they managed to get a few remedies for Carol's ailment.

Imagine bumping into the canon. Was that weird or what, and who was that he was with? All that concerned Erin was that he'd alert her family. Bloody hell, that was all she needed.

*

Once he had satisfied himself that the big Glasgow hardman was not scouring the cobbled streets of Marbella, O'Farrell dumped his current paramour and made his way back along the sea front. This could be the opportunity of a life time, but he would have to tread very carefully.

What could Erin Coyle be doing in Marbella with a small child? Whatever the circumstances, he had to get to her. She had to be stopped from alerting her father, it was just the sort of remark she would make. "Oh, you'll never guess who I just met, Canon O'Farrell and his boyfriend." Damn, that was all he needed.

For a seventy-year-old he could move, and he sprinted off down the street on the lookout for the two girls.

Amy spied the old man she'd bumped into and was jumping up and down and waving her little hand.

Erin motioned her to be quiet, but she was too late, they'd been spotted. Canon O'Farrell made his way through the packed street and caught up with his quarry.

"Well, well, how nice. We meet again, and who is this little cherub?" he asked stroking the wee one's hair.

"She's my friend's daughter, her mum's ill. We just came out to get her some medicine," wrote Erin.

"Oh, I must sit down, dear. I'm not feeling too well, it's the heat, you know."

"It's bloody Spain," thought Erin, who couldn't wait to get away.

"Come and sit beside me for a bit, just till I get my breath back," said the wily old man.

"I'm fursty, Erin, I'm fursty" said Amy, bouncing up and down on the sea wall. "I need to wee wee noooow."

"Look, you take her off to the ladies and sort her out. Leave your packages with me and I'll order us a cold drink."

"No, honest, it's fine. I need to get back to her mum."

"Ten minutes won't make any difference, and I should be okay by then."

Erin grabbed Amy by the hand and off they went to find a toilet, leaving their things with their companion.

They had only been gone a few minutes, but in that time the Canon had managed to procure two iced drinks, ice cream sundaes and a pot of tea. God, she thought, it would have taken half an hour just for someone to take her order. She laughed.

"So, my dear, what brings you back to Marbella so soon?"

Erin jerked up in surprise. How did he know she'd been in the resort before?

"Don't look so surprised, I was here when you were with your friends a few months ago."

It's a big place, she thought, and she was sure she hadn't seen him. Certainly not if he wore that gear all the time.

"In fact, you got quite friendly with my godson," he bluffed.

As Erin looked quizically at him, the priest went on. "Yes, my godson Bobby Mack, he's never stopped talking about you, he'll be delighted when I tell him you're in town," the canon lied blatantly. "Oh, but my dear, what a shame. The family are leaving in the morning, they're off to the States for a few weeks, what a shame you'll miss him."

Erin didn't know what to do, she wasn't sure if she entirely believed the man, but why would he lie? She had to see Bobby and Canon O'Farrell was her ticket.

"Do you think I could see him tonight before he leaves, Father?" She wrote. "It's very important."

"I don't know what he's doing tonight, probably out with his mates, but he's at home with Dianne just now, why don't you come on up to the villa with me?"

"I have to take Amy back and give Carol her medication. Could you wait for me? Or I could come up later, once I've seen to these guys?"

"Well, I suppose so, but I wouldn't leave it too long, Bobby waits around for no man, or woman, and this is his last night for some time. Remember, he wasn't expecting you, so he'll have plans."

"Wait for me," she wrote.

There was no way she could leave the little girl with a semi-conscious mother in a hotel room unsupervised. No, she had no choice.

Pity about the kid, mused Francis, she would have

fitted the bill perfectly. Well, not perfectly, his clients would have preferred something a little older, but once delivered there were never any complaints. He would see what he could do later, but his first priority was to cut off Erin Coyle from the outside world. He needed to think fast, something he had always prided himself on – it had helped him escape from a few scary situations over the years.

Capture

Bridget had phoned every clinic listed in the Yellow Pages with no luck; wherever her daughter had gone, she wasn't in one in the city. Unless, of course, she was using another name. If that was the case, Bridget knew she had no chance. She was just going to have to sit it out and hope that Paddy was too preoccupied to notice, but seriously, she didn't hold out much hope.

The man himself was certainly preoccupied at the moment. Paddy had committed, what was in his eyes, the cardinal sin. In his eagerness to get one over on O'Farrell, Paddy had strayed from his usual modus operandi. His naturally suspicious nature never allowed him to jump feet first into any situation; he always checked things out, looked from different perspectives and always, always had a 'Plan B', thus avoiding a capture or even arousing suspicion that he could be involved in anything suspect. But, in his haste to 'do' the canon, Paddy was now faced with a very dangerous situation.

So what did he have, he asked himself. He had a defunct computer; a bag with a substantial amount of cash and bonds which couldn't be traced; a key to a locker, a locker containing evidence of serious crimes committed by person or persons unknown with no definite link to O'Farrell.

What did he have to do to protect himself, the twins and Father Jack? The computer could be binned, but the cash and bonds? There was nothing to prove they were the proceeds of crime or that they belonged to anyone other than Paddy Coyle. The photographs could be destroyed as they were of no significant use. But the key and the contents of the locker were a different story. He had to relocate both and still ensure that they could be traced back to O'Farrell if need be. And that was the tricky part. Although Paddy had made up his mind that the man had taken his last holiday, he had to cover his tracks just in case . . .

The Kidnap

As she pulled on a fresh dress and vigorously brushed her hair, Erin thought this was not how she had planned her reunion with Bobby, but she had no time to do any more. She couldn't miss this opportunity — it seemed unlikely she'd get another. A quick check in the mirror, she'd have to do. One thing being pregnant had done for her, it certainly enhanced her breasts. For the first time in her life she didn't hanker after a boob job.

She'd tried to rouse her sick friend to no avail, the poor soul had been floored by whatever bug she'd been unlucky enough to catch and Erin thought she would recover quicker if they left her alone.

She scribbled a note saying 'Gone to meet Bobby. Had to take Amy, wish me luck. Erin.'

Taking the little girl by the hand, they ran back down to where they'd left Canon O'Farrell, but he was gone. Bugger, bugger, she swore in her head. They hadn't been gone that long, surely he could have waited? Erin felt like crying. She was desperate. If she couldn't see Bobby today, God only knew when they would meet up again.

Amy began squealing, "There he is, Erin, there he is," and sure enough, dozing in the shade was the missing priest.

"Sorry, ladies, I must have drifted off," smiled Canon O'Farrell. "Let's go, it's only a short stroll."

For most of the way the elderly man kept them entertained, telling funny little stories and winning them over. At home Erin had never liked the canon and had avoided him whenever possible, always finding him to be rude and stern, nothing like this man who was warm and funny and if only she knew; a damned good actor, so when he began subtly questioning her, she was completely taken in by him.

"What brings you to Marbella again, Erin?" He asked.

It was almost impossible to walk and write at the same time, so he became questioner and answerer.

"Was there a particular reason?" he cajoled. Seeing her blush, he pressed on. "It wasn't to do with a certain young man, was it?" Seeing Erin colour up again, he laughingly asked, "It wouldn't be my godson by any chance, would it?"

Erin shyly nodded her response.

"Oh dear, Erin, maybe I'm doing the wrong thing here. Maybe I shouldn't bring you to see Bobby, not when Dianne is with him. I don't think she'll make you very welcome. She's a tigress and Bobby is her baby, maybe we should forget it?"

Erin was vigorously shaking her head, she couldn't get this close and fail, she had to convince him to take her to the villa. Making her companions sit on the wall, Erin wrote, "I have to see him, it's very important."

"I'm sure it is, but I don't want to expose you and the little one to Dianne in a strop, and believe me, if she thought you were serious about her son, there would be murders. Let's face it, she put the kybosh on your romance earlier this year."

"What do you mean?"

"I told you, he never stopped talking about you."

"And she stopped him?"

"She did, so what do you think?"

"Remember who my dad is, I'm sure I'll cope."

As if he could forget who her father was. "Tell you what, why don't you wait in the pool house and I'll send Bobby down to you. I could always keep his mother occupied while you talk."

"Please, please. Thank you," she drew a bunch of kisses. God, that might not be appropriate for a priest, Erin thought.

Having safely ensconced his two charges in the pool house, Canon O'Farrell went off, as they thought, in search of Bobby.

The young man in question most certainly wasn't at home packing for a non-existent holiday to the States. He *was* on holiday, however. He and his three amigos had hired a motor cruiser and were just entering the marina in Majorca for the start of a few days of fishing and partying.

There was no chance of Bobby interfering with the house guests, invited or not.

The canon rummaged about in Dianne's medicine cabinet until he found what he was looking for. Back in the kitchen, he quickly squeezed fresh orange juice and loaded it with the crushed sleeping pills, working quickly in case Erin got inquisitive.

"I managed to get a quick word with Bobby and he's over the moon," said O'Farrell, laying down the tray of drinks.

"He was all for rushing straight down here, but I told him to wait till Dianne goes out. Shouldn't be more than half an hour, forty minutes, okay? Here, drink these, it gets quite hot in here and you certainly don't want to get dehydrated, especially the little one."

For some reason Erin suddenly felt intimidated by the canon. He seemed menacing now. Heavens, she told herself, she was being ridiculous. Only ten minutes ago he had been her saviour, telling her stories and promising to help her in her quest. But maybe he had worked out why she wanted to see Bobby and didn't approve, or was she just being paranoid? Whatever the reason, she was too tired to worry.

Voices drifted in and out of her consciousness, angry voices. She was sure somebody held her and forced her to drink something, but it was easy just to let the blackness take over.

The Breakup

Pete was surprised to find O'Farrell waiting for him when he got home from the club. The old man was usually well into the land of nod by the time he got in. There was something up and Pete knew he wasn't going to like it.

"You did what?" roared Pete Mack, smashing his fist on the marble counter top.

"It's only for a couple of days, till I get things organised," Frank cajoled his furious host, keeping his distance.

"Organised? You? You couldn't organise a piss-up in a brewery. No fucking way, get them out of my house now."

"How? Sling her over my shoulder and saunter down to the marina and hope the local Caribeneros don't notice me?"

"Don't be so fucking smart, I can't believe you brought Paddy Coyle's daughter back to my gaff, drugged her and then tell me you're about to fucking hold her to ransom! Fuck me, you really are a piece of work."

"What did you want me to do, Pete? She recognised me. Do you think she was going to forget she'd seen her parish priest dressed to the nines and holding hands with a boy as black as coal? I'm pretty sure her next phone call home would start, 'you'll never guess who I just met?'"

"I don't give a fuck. You should never have brought her here. This is some fucking mess, I'm telling you, and what about the kid?"

"What about her? She's the reason I brought them here. She'll fill the last consignment, nobody so far knows they're missing, it's heaven sent."

"I'll fucking heaven sent you, you stupid bastard. For the past ten years I've kept everything together, tied up every loose end and made sure nothing could be traced back to here, or to us, and in one fell swoop you've compromised everything. When this is over you are fucking done, man. I'm telling you, done!" Pete stormed into the house and picked up the phone.

All had gone better than the canon had expected. Pete, anxious to get rid of his unwanted guests had no choice, the priest was confident they would get away with this. His partner was right though, it was time to call it a day.

As Carol got back into bed she found the note left by Erin. Thank God Amy was being looked after. She swallowed the medication and fell promptly back to sleep. She certainly would not have slept so soundly if she had had any idea of the danger her precious daughter and friend found themselves in.

Pete was on the phone for the best part of an hour, during which time his temper and anger had worsened rather than abated. Endeavouring to reopen channels he had recently closed, and closed in such a way that prevented situations like this, he really didn't know if it could be done. Erin Coyle was a problem, but if all else failed she'd sleep with the fish. Pete had no qualms about disposing of her; the problem was the canon and the link back to him.

"Frank, you do realise that Paddy Coyle will come and it'll be either him or us? He won't let us walk away from this, not where his daughter's concerned."

"Well, we'll have to be ready for him. She's the only bargaining tool we have to make him return my money."

"You might not get the opportunity to spend it," sneered Pete. "My advice would have been to walk away, but it's too late now, you've already sullied his name and dramatic though this sounds, it's going to be a fight to the death."

"It would be that with or without his daughter. He knows too much and wouldn't rest until he'd exposed us. At least this way we have a fighting chance."

"You may as well get some sleep; tomorrow will be a long, long day."

The Call

Carol had no idea what time she woke, but the sun was high in the sky and from the balcony, she could see that most of the loungers around the pool were occupied. She was still a bit shaky, but a hundred times better than she had been yesterday. Obviously it had been one of those shitty twenty-four hour things; she wasn't okay, but she could face the day.

Looking around the room it was apparent that neither Amy nor Erin's beds had been slept in. Carol was a little perturbed. After a quick shower she made her way to the dining room, but breakfast was long over. She scoured the pool area for her daughter and friend. No sign of either. Next, the play area and the gardens but there was still no sign of them.

By now it was mid-morning and Carol knew that Erin was far too responsible to keep her little girl out overnight, and certainly not until almost lunchtime the next day. Panic was beginning to kick in. Oh my

God, had something happened? An accident? Had they gotten stuck somewhere? Had Bobby gone mad and done them some mischief? She had to find them. She had a really bad feeling about this.

Grabbing hold of one of the holiday reps, she gave a garbled account of what was wrong.

"You have to call the police; they've been gone for hours. Check the hospitals in case there's been an accident."

"Hang on, hang on, don't panic. When did you last see your friend and daughter?" The uninterested young girl had heard this or a similar story a dozen times already this season. They always turned up, usually still half-cut from the night before. Mind you, they didn't usually take a four-year-old along for company, but there was no accounting for some folk.

"I'm not sure. I think it was early evening. I was ill in bed and they went for something to make me feel better. I vaguely remember them coming back and I found a note saying that she was going to meet a guy. She had Amy with her and to wish her luck."

"There you go then," smiled the girl. "She's not missing. She's just not back yet."

"For God's sake, they've been away for hours."

"They could have gone clubbing, some of the clubs don't close till about now."

"With a four-year-old in tow? Don't be so bloody ridiculous." snapped the distraught mother. "I want you to call the police now. My child and my friend are missing."

With great reluctance, the sullen rep made a few calls, furious at all the paperwork she was going to have to complete, and still adamant that the pair would turn up any minute.

It took almost an hour before two equally disinterested Civil Guards, who looked like they would have trouble sorting out a parking ticket, arrived.

Carol didn't have much information for them to go on; all she knew was that Bobby cleaned pools and had something to do with a nightclub. It was now almost twenty-four hours since she had last seen the pair and she was frantic. The officers took a few notes, asked a few questions, and then left, leaving the terrified mother at a loss as to what was happening.

Desperately searching through Erin's bag for any clues, Carol came across her friend's phone. They needed help and it didn't look like it was going to come from the Spanish authorities or the holiday firm. No matter how much Erin didn't want her family to know about the pregnancy, this was way beyond keeping the secret. They had to be told.

"Erin, is that you? God, child, I've been almost out of my mind with worry," her mother cried with relief.

Paddy had insisted on his daughter having a phone for emergencies. In order to overcome her problem, she had only to ring once for yes and twice for no. This simple code allowed her to keep in touch with any of her family or friends.

"Mrs Coyle, this isn't Erin." A young woman was sobbing into her daughter's phone.

"Who are you? Where's Erin?" Bridget demanded.

"I don't know. She's missing with my daughter."

"What do you mean missing and why is she with your daughter?" Eventually Bridget got the story from a completely distraught Carol, who by now was in bits.

"I need to get my husband. Keep this phone with you all the time. Do not go anywhere without it and make sure it's charged. I'll phone back as soon as I get him."

"I'm so sorry, I did try to talk her out of it but she wouldn't have it. My Amy's only four, she's just a baby. Dear God, I'll die if anything happens to her." Carol sobbed.

Much as Bridget wanted to comfort and assure the girl, she had no words. Her daughter was missing too.

Sick with worry, she had to get Paddy. If only it had been an abortion, at least they'd know she was safe. It took her nearly half an hour to reach him and relay the telephone call. He got back home in record time.

"Are you sure it's not some sick joke?" he asked, clutching at straws.

"I don't think so, she sounded genuine enough to me, and even if it is, we can't take the chance and ignore it."

"Get me on the next flight to Alicante."

"What about the twins? Don't you think you should have backup?" Bridget was concerned that Paddy on his own would create bedlam, whereas if his brothers were with him, he would be less likely to land up in a Spanish jail.

"Not both, somebody needs to stay here and take care of things."

"Okay, I'll book Michael," said Bridget, going to answer the phone. "I'm sorry, Father Jack, he's busy right now. Well, if it's that urgent, okay. Paddy, Father Jack is on the phone, he says it's urgent."

"Tell him I'll speak to him later. Nothing is more urgent than this."

Listening to what the caller had to say Bridget handed the phone to Paddy, "You better hear this."

Paddy was silent throughout the call, his face thunderous. It had been a long time since Bridget had seen that expression.

"Mrs Gavin's gone. She packed up and disappeared in the night. Paddy, she'd lived at St. Jude's for nigh on twenty years and all that was left was a note."

"What did it say?"

"Tell Paddy Coyle if he wants to see his daughter again, phone this number."

"Christ, we've just had a call from Spain saying she's disappeared along with a young kid."

"You know what that means? They've got another consignment, but why involve Erin?"

"God knows," was his reply as he dialled the number.

The phone was answered on the first ring. Whoever it was had been waiting for the call.

"You got my message then, Coyle?"

"You know you are a dead man?"

"I know where your precious daughter is and I'm willing to sell this information for the contents of the safety deposit box."

"Where are you?"

"Spain, that's all you need to know for now."

"Fuck's sake, man, I need to book a flight."

"Alicante. Ring me when you arrive." The line went dead.

"Paddy, there are no flights from Glasgow today and it would be standby only tomorrow."

"Forget it, I can't sit about in an airport when my daughter is in danger. Get me Ritchie. He owes me a favour and I'm calling it in."

Paddy had known Ritchie Scott for years, since not long after the young fella got his pilot's licence. He now owned a small air courier business, operating out of Glasgow and was doing well for himself. That hadn't been the case a few years ago when he had unwittingly been used to courier drugs to and from the continent for some seriously heavy villains. Thanks to the intervention of Paddy, the courier wasn't found floating face down in the River Clyde.

"Hello Ritchie, Paddy Coyle here. I need a favour."

"Hi Paddy, what's up?"

"Ritchie, I need to get to Spain right now. All the commercial flights are full and I'm desperate. The clock's ticking and believe me, every second counts."

"Okay, where exactly in Spain?"

"I need to get to Marbella."

"A private landing strip or commercial?"

"Private, and as near as possible."

"How many passengers?"

"This leg just two."

"Nothing illegal being carried?"

"No drugs, if that's what you're asking."

"Firearms?"

"Don't ask."

"Okay, I didn't hear that. What about return flights?"

"Tomorrow. Hopefully with three other passengers."

"Do you need a car?"

"Yep."

"When do you want to leave?"

"I can be at the airport in twenty minutes."

"No problem, I'll take you myself. See you in half an hour or so."

Bridget had already called Michael and he was on his way to the airport. Paddy's bag was packed; he filled Sean in on what was happening and what business needed to be taken care of. From the call to being airborne was a record ninety minutes.

They arrived in Spain just over three hours later and the two men headed straight into town to see Erin's companion.

"You must be Carol?" Paddy addressed the tear-ravaged young woman. "Tell me everything you know, do not miss anything out. My Erin's a resourceful girl. She'll be fine and your daughter couldn't be with anyone better."

Oh how Carol wished she believed this rhetoric.

She described her first encounter with Erin in the department store and how the girl had been in a terrible state. About their meeting the following day and how Carol had begged her to tell her family, she herself having once been in the same predicament. But Erin had been adamant she had to deal with this herself. Her plan had been to confront the father and take it from there. Everything seemed so childish when relating it to this huge man, but at the time it had been a reasonably coherent plan.

Carol had little or no information other than the bare details concerning the potential father, and as she had been completely bedridden since their arrival, where they had gone or who they met was a mystery. All she had was the scribbled note saying 'gone to meet Bobby, taking Amy, wish me luck.'

Paddy tried to get her to remember anything about the time they had arrived, when Erin had gone for medication, anything she could recall, but she drew a blank.

"Now, I want you to stay here in case she phones or comes back. This is my number if you hear anything or remember anything. Phone me and I'll keep you up to date."

Carol felt slightly better knowing that Erin's father was on the case, he would find them. Please God, don't let it be too late.

Paddy's next stop was to meet with two of the Costa's main men: Charlie Taylor and Philip the Greek Manson. He'd had a few dealings with both men over the years and though reluctant to put himself in their debt, he had no choice. Within five minutes he had the name, address and heads up on the Bobby fella. It seemed he was a serial player in the resort. Young, good-looking, flash, and his father owned one of the hottest clubs in the town.

"I have to say, Paddy, not a family I would have thought would be mixed up in our world," said Phil the Greek. "The man is no mug and runs a good gaff, but he seems as straight as."

"I always thought the wife wore the trousers in that partnership. Some gal is Dianne Mack, balls of steel," laughed Charlie. "Up for anything, she is, and she's warmed a few beds around town."

Paddy Coyle looked like he'd been slapped. Pete and Dianne? No way. Mack! That was some coincidence. Christ, how many times had he and the family holidayed here in Marbella and all that time his worst enemy was operating right under his nose? That and the bastard O'Farrell, what a team.

"Are you thinking what I'm thinking?" Michael quizzed Paddy.

"Too much of a coincidence, wouldn't you say?" replied his brother. "Thanks, gentlemen, you've been a great help and I owe you one."

"It's on the house, mate. Good luck."

First stop was the Marbella Princess, but apart from a couple of cleaning staff there was no sign of their quarry.

"Look, Paddy, don't go in like John Wayne. Let's suss the place out first," Michael pleaded on their arrival at Mack's villa. "We've got the edge on them, there's no way they're going to have a clue we're in town already. They probably think we're still standing in the Globespan queue, waiting to check our bags in. I reckon they'll think they have at least another five or six hours before we arrive, so let's use it."

The Dark

Fighting through the layers of blackness, Erin tried hard to come to. She knew instinctively this wasn't normal, this wasn't just sleepy. How long had she been like this and more to the point, how the hell did she get like this? She needed to concentrate, but still she floated in and out of consciousness.

Everything was jumbled, but at least the angry voices had gone. Could that mean she had been dumped and left on her own? Which was worse? My God, she felt like she'd been hit by a truck. Was that it, had she had an accident? Nothing made sense.

The pitch black weighed down on her, but she could hear breathing and small whimpering noises, like an animal or a small child. Amy, it must be Amy, somewhere in this darkness. How to reach the little girl? Erin could barely move, she was bound tight. Who would want to keep them prisoner? All these unanswered questions. Panic was beginning to kick in.

At first the blackness seemed impenetrable, but her eyes were growing accustomed to the dark and she could make out shapes. She seemed to be in a storeroom and was pretty sure she was on a mattress. Her foot touched something and Amy gave a little grunt. The little girl obviously hadn't come to yet.

She recalled Canon O'Farrell going to get Bobby. He had left them in a little cabana by the swimming pool, but that was all she remembered. Except for all the shouting. But who had been shouting and why? She hadn't a clue. Where was the canon? Had something happened to him, was he in here too? She could only hear one other person breathing, so what did that mean?

The only thought in her head was to get free, but whatever her captor had used to bind her was tearing her poor wrists to bits, at even the feeblest attempts to break free, She could feel the blood trickling through her fingers. This was no good; she needed something sharp, or to free Amy. If only she could reach her and get the little girl to understand what she wanted her to do.

Amy was regaining consciousness. She was very distressed and sobbing uncontrollably for her mum. Erin edged her way over to her, but the closer she got the further away Amy shrank from the figure in the dark and the louder her screams became. Desperate to comfort the child, but unable to communicate, Erin backed away from her, hoping she would realise who it was and not some bogeyman. Although she herself wasn't so sure the bogeyman wasn't waiting behind the door for them. What could she do to get free?

Erin tried to get near to Amy once more and set the poor child off into another wave of terrified shrieks. This was useless and might bring their captors all the quicker. Whatever the reason for their kidnap, they stood a far better chance untied than bound like Christmas turkeys. What could she do to make the child understand?

Over the years since she had lost her voice Erin had tried and failed at every attempt to make a noise. The only sound she had ever accomplished was a most peculiar and bizarre method of whistling. It was so much of a hit or miss that she'd long since given up on it. There was nothing else for it, so with all her concentration, she managed a few blows. Amy stopped crying for a few seconds, long enough for Erin to cover her entire repertoire of sucks and blows and weird noises.

Total silence. No crying, just silence and then there was the tiniest chuckle. Erin edged her way over to Amy's corner and with a gentle prod the child threw her arms round Erin's neck. Now the hard bit, she thought. How the hell do I get her to understand what I want her to do? But this was one smart four-year-old. Sitting back to back Erin managed to loosen Amy's bonds and without too much pain set her free.

It took some time for the nimble little fingers to pick the tape undone, and all in the dark, but eventually both girls were free. Terrified, Erin opened the door and cautiously peeked outside. The pool area was deserted and she grabbed Amy by the hand. They sprinted across the terrace and into the scrubland beyond. They were met with an insurmountable high wall topped with barbed wire. No way out there. The two escapees stealthily worked their way round the edge of the property, petrified of being discovered, but hoping for some means of escape.

"I'll go and check on them in a few minutes." Pete was busy making up a new batch of juice. "They'll be coming round fairly soon and I have to be careful how much I give the kid."

"We should be hearing from Coyle shortly. By my reckoning he should arrive in the next hour or so. By the time he clears customs and gets into town, that batch should see us through. I take it the cruiser is primed and ready for the off?"

"Of course it is, what do you think I've been doing for the past hour, sitting on my arse?"

"No need to get antsy, I was simply asking." The last thing O'Farrell wanted to do was piss off Pete. He knew he was treading on very shaky ground.

Just talking to this old fucker made his blood boil. Whatever the outcome of this night, Canon Francis O'Farrell would not see another dawn. Pete had had enough. Win or lose he was finished with him. Having spent most of the morning and early afternoon preparing for the coming visit, as far as Pete was concerned Paddy Coyle's comeuppance had been a long time in the making.

"They've gone," he roared at the priest. "They've fucking escaped, you old goat. How could you be

214

trumped by a four-year-old and a fucking mute? I do not believe it."

"Don't be stupid, they can't have gone. They must be here somewhere, check again."

Pete couldn't make up his mind whether to fucking brain the idiot or go and check again for the two hostages. Fuck it, he'd do both, but the pool house was nearest so he'd keep until later. Amidst the chaos, neither man noticed the silver Mercedes draw up and park opposite.

The runaways had managed to squeeze through the tiniest of holes into a neighbouring property. They could hear dogs, big dogs; the breed of dogs that patrol grounds and would attack anything that strayed into their territory. No way could they go back and if they went closer to the house they would be savaged. Erin needed to find them somewhere safe to hide. Crawling cautiously along the extreme perimeter of the neighbouring garden, so as not to alert the beasts, they made their way down to the water's edge. Miracle upon miracle, there was an old battered rowing boat bobbing about. As quick as they could they both climbed in, pulling the tarpaulin over their heads. They would wait until the hue and cry had died down a bit and then make their getaway.

In for the kill

There was no doubting who Pete Mack was; it was like turning back the clock. Paddy had to admit the years had been good to McClelland. He was tanned, distinguished, and from the look of the villa, certainly not short of a bob or two. A far cry from the piss-poor ragamuffin who ran alongside Paddy on the rob, or who had spent twelve months in Polmont Young Offenders only to come out and stitch his best mate up well and truly.

Paddy couldn't believe how seeing McClelland after all these years still affected him. The bile rose in his throat, his hatred was almost palpable. He wanted to rip his fucking head off. To think that yet again this bastard may have harmed his only child. Well, this time there was no reprieve, no mercy; he would finish him off with his bare hands.

"Did you get a look at him?" asked Michael, interrupting Paddy's thoughts.

"Oh, I did that, bro. Him and his bum chum. That

fucking little weasel, poncing about like something from *Hawaii Five O*. I can't wait to get a grip on that one," snarled his brother.

"There's something up though, Paddy. Look at them, they're running about like bloody headless chickens, look."

Sure enough, the two men appeared to be searching for something or someone and were bitterly arguing between themselves. They entered the small building at the end of the terrace.

"Perfect," whispered Paddy, "let's go, Mikey."

The brothers positioned themselves on either side of the entrance. First one out was O'Farrell, who they caught completely by surprise. He didn't know what had hit him as he slumped to the ground.

Still ranting and raving, McClelland followed, stumbling over the inert form of O'Farrell and cursing even louder. A glimpse of his assailant confirmed yet again that he had underestimated Paddy Coyle.

Michael secured the two men using the same ligatures that had been used on his niece and Amy. There was no way either of them could escape. Meanwhile Paddy searched the villa from top to bottom, but no sign of either girl.

First to regain conscientiousness was Pete, looking down the barrel of a gun.

"Well, Paddy, long time no see. You're looking well," said Pete at his smarmiest.

Paddy couldn't help himself. He smashed McClelland across the mouth, dislodging some very expensive bridge work and at the very least dislocating the man's jaw.

"That's just for starters," he snarled. "Now where is my daughter, you piece of shit?"

"Would you believe me if I told you truthfully, I don't know?" came the reply.

"Fucking truthfully? You don't know the meaning of the word. I'll ask you again, where is my daughter?"

"And again I'll tell you truthfully, I don't know." This reply resulted in even more work for the orthodontist and most definitely his jaw was broken.

During this interlude O'Farrell had come to and having quickly assessed the situation, he knew instinctively that if Coyle thought that they didn't have the girl, or didn't know her whereabouts, then they were both dead.

"She's not here, Paddy. You don't for one minute think we'd keep her here? Now, let's be adult about this. I have no reason to harm Erin and she's of no use to me, so you produce the money and we're quits."

"Erm, am I getting this right? You're telling me what you're prepared to do? Has the fact that you're my prisoner slipped your mind? Neither of you are in any position to bargain."

"Oh, I think you're a bit out on that score," said the old man. "We all know that you're not likely to let us walk from here so what have we got to lose? Why should we tell you where your daughter and her little friend are? All I will say is they won't last more than a couple of hours. At which point the tide will come in and they might last five or ten terrifying minutes before leaving this mortal coil. Neither, I might add, as good Catholic girls, having received the last rights.

218

Now that really would upset Bridget and Lizzie."

Michael had to physically restrain Paddy as he pummelled the old priest relentlessly. "Tell me where she is, you old bastard. Tell me now," but O'Farrell had again passed out.

McClelland had toughened up over the years, but he was still no match against a fighting machine like Paddy Coyle.

"Don't listen to that stupid old fucker," his ex-best mate pleaded. "I'm telling you, Paddy, we don't have them. They got away. Hard to believe? A four-year-old and a mute got one over on us. But they did, that's how you were able to capture us. We were more interested in finding them than in your arrival."

Paddy walked over to where Michael was standing guard. "What do you think? Could they really have got away?"

"Christ man, she's your daughter and no matter how much cotton wool you wrap her up in, she's still going to come up trumps. The girl's a survivor. I say we finish this pair off, not that it will take much for our beloved canon, and go look for her. She can't be far. What the fuck is up with those dogs? You don't think . . .?"

Paddy took off.

Intervention

The reception area was pretty quiet when Sam made her last call of the day. Jesus, that poor female was still hanging about and that face would put anyone off their dinner. Shit, it looked like her kid hadn't turned up yet. She really should go and speak to her. It was just that kids went missing every bloody week and she'd spend hours searching for them, just to have them turn up after a few hours sporting new tattoos or off their faces on the latest drug of choice.

"Hello, no word yet?" Tact was not one of her strong points. "Have the police been back in touch?"

Carol was almost incoherent, crying and talking at the same time. "No-one. I'm nearly out of my mind. I have to do something, I can't sit about here any longer, but I have no idea where to start."

"Shit," thought Sam. Maybe she should have taken this more seriously. "Tell me what you know."

"Just that my friend was going to meet a guy she'd had a thing with in the summer."

"Right, but how is the child involved?"

"I was ill and she had to look after her."

"What do you know about the boyfriend and where was she meeting him?"

"His name is Bobby and he cleans pools."

"Fuck, she's not after Bobby Mack?" Sam laughed. "This is a small town and there's not a female in Marbella he's not promised the earth to. As far as the tourists go, he tells them all he wants them to stay and have his babies."

"Well she believed him."

"Hang on, let me make a couple of calls." She walked off.

A few minutes later she returned. "Right, I've got his address, let's go." She jumped on her tiny scooter. "Come on, we've wasted enough time, it's not far," and off they sped.

"I'm not sure exactly which house, but we'll just ring them all till we get him."

She pressed the intercom, "Hi, Pizza Express. I've got a delivery for Bobby Mack."

"Wrong house. You want Glendale, three down on the left," the disembodied voice replied.

There was no reply to the buzzer, but the two girls could hear shouting and loud voices, so whether the occupants liked it or not, they were about to have visitors.

Bloody hell, thought Sam, I could lose my job. So what? She was a bloody good rep and she'd get another one easily enough.

So much for high-tech security systems, the girls climbed up and over the gates and within minutes they were both in.

There had obviously been a break-in, a robbery, or whatever. There were two unconscious, badly beaten men tied up on the patio and blood was everywhere. The older man was bad, really bad; in fact Sam was sure he was a goner.

The other was coming round.

"Help me," he urged. "Help me. Get me out of this before they get away." Noticing that Carol was on the phone the injured man called out, "No police. No police or they'll harm the child. Get me free."

"Where's my daughter? What have you done to her? Tell me now!" she screamed.

"I haven't done anything to her. It's the others. For fuck's sake, get me out of this lot before it's too late."

Carol ran to the outdoor kitchen, picked the sharpest knife from the rail and proceeded to cut the binding.

Despite his injuries, the younger of the two men grabbed something that had fallen on the floor and sprinted off in the direction of next door's property.

A bloodcurdling scream stopped both Sam and Carol in their strides. Fuck, what had they got into? Carol knew there was no doubt that the scream came from Amy and she was in serious trouble. She needed her mother.

Still holding the knife, she ran for her life in the direction of the noise. God help whoever had made her child scream because she would gut them from end to end if they'd harmed her most precious possession.

Housetrained

Her nerves were shot to pieces. She was like a coiled spring; terrified the dogs would get their scent or that their captors would find them. Let's face it, she thought to herself, it wouldn't be that difficult, but it was the best hiding place she could find.

Fortunately, thanks to the gentle bobbing of the boat, Amy had been lulled back to sleep and for the time being had stopped her sobbing. The only real chance they stood was to keep absolutely quiet, but the poor wee soul was distraught, if only she could last a little longer.

She could hear scraping and, too scared to look, Erin pulled Amy closer to her. The scraping was getting more frantic, one of the dogs was investigating the boat. His kennel-mates were running to and fro at the water's edge, ready to attack at any moment.

A wet, slobbering head poked its way under the tarpaulin, eye to eye with Erin. For what seemed like hours, the dog and the girl stared each other out, both ready to strike. With all the strength she could muster Erin smashed the vicious brute across his snout with one of the oars. Yelping, it flew back to the water's edge as the other two bounded through the water to the boat, snarling and growling.

Endeavouring to cover the child, Erin wrapped Amy in the tarp as quickly as she could, leaving no protection for herself. Wielding the oar, she smashed and thrashed at the dogs, but it was a losing battle. One of the beasts had managed to grab Amy's arm from under her covering and was pulling the child out of the boat.

The noise of the barking and snarling beasts was incredible, then a shot rang out and then another. Silence. Erin collapsed in a heap.

"Erin, Erin, it's okay, it's me, Dad. You're safe, Erin."

The blackness washed over her again, but this time she didn't want to fight it. She didn't want to face what was out there. She must have died. Why else would she be able to hear her dad? He was at home, not here in Spain.

She could hear lots of other voices. That was uncle Michael, how could she hear him? Someone was lifting her out of the boat. She knew who it was, she recognised his smell. It *was* him, he'd come to save her. What about Amy, was she safe? Please don't let her have been mauled by the dogs, let her be safe. Warily Erin opened her eyes. It *was* her dad and uncle Michael. Carol was tending to Amy, but why was that man pointing a gun at them? Why were her dad and Michael just ignoring him? He was going to shoot. She was watching him intently. He knew she was watching and he smiled just as he pulled the trigger.

"Noooooooooo!"

Where did the warning come from? Who had saved his life? They were all dumbstruck. As he looked down at his daughter, the big Glasgow hard man had tears streaming down his face.

"Erin, you spoke. You shouted. Please tell me I'm not imagining it."

"Uh huh," replied his daughter. Her voice was husky and sounded like a rusty old machine. But it was a voice nonetheless.

The gunman laughed and then the most peculiar expression crossed his face: both surprise and bewilderment as he slumped to the ground.

Carol pulled the knife from between his shoulder blades. "He shouldn't have hurt Amy," was all she said.

The Last Rites

"Michael, we have to work fast. We need to get Erin, the kid and her mother out of here."

Paddy nodded in agreement. "Hey you, blondie," he called to the holiday rep. "You look as if you've got a bit about you. I want you to get them back to the hotel, call the missing persons off, say they turned up or something. Then come straight back here and wait for us, okay?"

Shit! Sam had been on the verge of disappearing back over the gate. She'd done what she set out to do, and anyway, this scene was far too heavy for her. But when the big man collared her she certainly wasn't going to be disobeying. You never know, with a bit of luck she might come out of this a bit better off. Sam had learned a long time ago to look after number one. Just as long as the mother didn't let on that she maybe should have acted sooner. That was a chance she'd have to take.

They left the villa the way they'd entered. Sam

bundled the shocked and traumatised passengers into the Mercedes and headed back to town. Luckily, there were few guests around when they arrived at the hotel and they passed through reception and into the lift without arousing any interest.

The rep carried out Paddy's instructions and waited while Carol contacted the local police and called off the non-existent manhunt. Thank God they'd taken matters into their own hands if this was how missing persons were dealt with. Sam ordered room service and made sure her charges had everything they needed before heading off to collect Paddy and the other big man.

Much to Paddy's regret he certainly had given the old man a hammering. He was annoyed with himself, reckoning O'Farrell had got off lightly as he aimed one more vicious kick at the inert form. How he would've liked him to suffer, just as the merchandise he had traded in had suffered. He had no-one to blame but himself and his legendary temper. It had been a long time since he had vented that on anyone.

Paddy loaded O'Farrell into the cruiser and headed round to the neighbouring mooring where Michael was waiting to stow his passenger on board. How the mighty had fallen. The dapper, well-dressed man about town was going to his watery grave. Not in a fine oak casket and draped in a silk shroud, mourned by many, but tied up in an old, filthy tarpaulin, mourned by none.

The brothers headed out to sea with their silent cargo. McClelland was first overboard. There was a loud splash and Paddy's old mate disappeared from view. Paddy felt nothing.

Michael had already hoisted O'Farrell onto the rail when the body groaned.

"Fuck, Paddy, he's still alive," said Michael, almost letting go.

"Good," said Paddy, peering into the face of the most despicable creature he had ever come across in his life. "Good. I want mine to be the last face he ever sees before entering the gates of hell." He laughed as he stared right into the old man's eyes and saw the terror in them.

The shock of the cold water brought him immediately to his senses. As he surfaced, he saw the cruiser disappear into the distance.

Meet the Wife

As they secured the cruiser back in its moorings, the brothers were eager to get off the premises and away from the crime scene. It amused Paddy that despite the number of gunshots, no-one had come to investigate or called the police. This was an area where if something didn't involve you, you didn't get involved.

Five more minutes and they would have been home and dry. As they sprinted across the terrace, Paddy and Michael were suddenly blinded by the full blare of the security lights and a strident, disembodied Scottish voice yelled at them from just inside the house. "What the fuck are you doing on my property and who the fuck are you?"

Paddy couldn't see a thing, but he recognised the woman immediately; the voice said it all. "Hello, Dianne, enjoy your trip? I'm afraid the welcome home party have left," he laughed.

"Jesus! Paddy Coyle," said the stunned owner of the voice.

"So you remember me? I'm flattered."

"Pete!" She screamed. "Pete, get your arse out here now."

"You'll have to shout a bit louder than that darlin', he's well out of earshot."

"Where's my husband? What the hell have you done with him?" Dianne roared at the two men.

"Pete? Oh, Pete's gone skinnydipping. Him and his best pal."

"Skinnydipping? What have you done to them?" wailed Dianne. "Why, Paddy? Why, after all these years? Why could you not leave us alone?"

"My daughter, that's why."

"Your daughter? What about her?"

"I'll get to her in a minute." Quite nonchalantly Paddy turned to his brother, "Michael, go and get the car keys off blondie and send her back to the hotel. This might take a little time. Sit down, Dianne. We need to have a little chat."

"Chat? A fucking chat?" Hysteria was rising in her voice. "Oh, I'll be chatting alright, chatting with the carabineri, the National Guard, Interpol. The fucking lot."

"That's not a good idea, Dianne. I want you to listen before you make any rash decisions," said Paddy quite amicably, although it was obvious from his demeanour that he was feeling anything but amicable.

"Don't think you scare me, you fucking two-bit crook."

"Language, Dianne. That's not very ladylike."

"Where the fuck is everyone? Bobby, where's Bobby? Where's my son? By Christ, he had better be okay."

"Shut up, for fuck's sake, woman. There's no-one else but us on the premises. Your darling Pete stupidly made sure of that, and as for Bobby, I've not laid eyes on that young buck, but trust me, when I do, he may well be keeping his father company."

This was definitely the wrong thing to say to the incensed mother. Dianne was like a woman possessed. The thought of anyone threatening to harm her only son was more than she could endure. She flew off the sofa, gouging at Paddy's face with her beautifully manicured talons.

It took all of Michael's strength to pull her off his brother and he received a few battle scars himself in the process. Christ, she was some woman.

A swift sharp slap stunned her into silence. "This is your last chance, lady, or so help me God, you'll suffer the same fate. Now shut up and listen to me." Paddy shook her. "Your beloved husband and that lairy little Irish cunt are a right pair of nonces. For the past ten years or so they've been making a bloody fortune running the biggest paedophile ring in Europe. And before you say you don't believe me, I *know* you know all about it."

"Prove it," snarled the woman.

"Oh, I've got the proof alright and one word in a certain person's ear and the hottest club in town will be colder than a witch's tit. You'll be ruined, finished, and I suspect, possibly run out of town."

"Don't be ridiculous. Nobody will believe a word of it. We're well respected in this town. Everybody knows Pete and Dianne Mack."

"Don't kid yourself, sweetheart. When word of this gets out, there'll be a queue of 'friends' around the block, ready to help you pack. Trust me. The big guns here will turn a blind eye to most activities. A bit of smuggling, guns, drugs, even sex workers. They don't even mind a bit of murder or extortion. But when it comes to kids, the gloves are off and no-one will believe that you didn't know all about it."

Dianne was losing some of her bravado. She knew from the past that Paddy Coyle would think nothing of finishing her off, but she had to keep face, it was her only chance.

"Okay, so I had my suspicions," she volunteered. "That's why I was sent back home. I refused to breathe the same air as that odious little fucker. So I gave Pete an ultimatum. Frank or me."

"Who the fuck is Frank?" asked Michael.

"O'Farrell. He likes to be called Frank when he's in his civvies. Anyway, Pete promised me this was the last time, so I buggered off and left them to it. But I don't understand how your daughter got mixed up in all this."

"We don't know the full story, but it seems she came back to Marbella to hook up with some little fucker she met over the summer. Some guy who promised her they'd live happily ever after, just to get into her pants. Ring any bells?"

Dianne blanched. She'd warned him for years

that some day it would come back and bite him on his smooth, tanned, rounded arse. And it had, in the shape of Paddy Coyle.

"Somehow she seems to have got caught up with that old bastard. Maybe she recognised him, I don't know, but he and Pete kept her and her mate's kid prisoner and tried to blackmail me."

"For fuck's sake, what a pair of idiots."

"So, your choice. You keep your mouth shut. No police. You know nothing, you've just come back from a trip home. Michael and I are heading back to the hotel and we'll be away early morning. If there are any repercussions, I will personally come back and finish you both off and you *know* that's no idle threat."

"Not much of a choice, is it?" murmured Dianne.

"Oh, I don't know. You're a very rich woman now. A very rich, single woman."

She was arranging the funeral in her head before Paddy and Michael got into the car.

Homecoming

"Hello, Mum." The voice on the other end of the phone was barely distinguishable, like metal grating on metal.

"Who's that? Carol is that you?" Bridget shouted into the mouthpiece. "Speak to me! What's happening?"

Again the raspy voice, "It's me, Mum. Erin."

"Oh my god. OH MY GOD," she screamed as tears streamed down her face. "Is it really you, darling? Speak to me, say something else."

"Yes, it's really me," Erin laughed, handing the phone over to Carol.

Bridget couldn't take in what she'd just heard. Had Erin just spoken? It had been ten long years since she'd heard her daughter speak, never mind laugh. Dear God, what had happened to bring this miracle about?

"Hello, hello, Mrs Coyle. It's Carol, it's okay, she's safe and no real harm done."

"What do you mean no real harm? What harm did they suffer? It had to be something dreadful to shock her into getting her speech back."

"Honestly, she's fine. Do you want to speak to her again?"

Bridget composed herself and listened to something she never thought she'd hear again: her beloved daughter.

"Mum, it's quite painful for me to speak, so you have to believe me, everybody's fine and we'll be home early morning, okay? Love you."

That simple phrase just broke her mother up. Not since she was eight years old had Erin Coyle been able to say what most mothers cherish. "Love you back," said Bridget in floods of tears, but for the first time in a long, long while, tears of joy.

"Are you feeling a bit happier?" Carol asked.

"I am, dear. Goodness, I never asked. I take it your wee one is safe and well?"

"Yes, she's fine. She seems none the worse for her ordeal. She's jumping about on the bed, demanding food. I'm the one that's in a state. I can't stop thinking about what could have happened to them. I don't think I've stopped crying for the past couple of hours."

"It's the shock, you'll be fine. I just thank God you were with Erin. God knows what could have happened." Both mothers dissolved into tears once more.

"Where's Paddy? Let me speak to him," blubbered Bridget.

"He's not back yet, but I'll get him to ring as soon as he gets here."

A knock on the door heralded the appearance of Sam the holiday rep. "I think I just got the sack," the blonde girl laughed. "My bosses think I was out on the lash and just didn't turn up for work."

"If only," Carol engulfed her in a bear hug.

"Can you imagine their reaction if I told them the truth? Sorry I missed the pub crawl earlier, but I was helping clear up a crime scene. Christ, not only would I get the sack, I'd be bloody deported," she roared with laughter.

She was just what the sombre little party needed to take their minds off what they had all gone through in the past couple of days.

"Thank you," said Carol. "Seriously, I can't thank you enough."

"Hey, don't mention it, it's all in a day's work. Well, I hope I've still got a day's work," Carol shrugged off her predicament. "What about Bobby Mack? What are you going to do about him?" she asked Erin.

"Not much I can do," replied Erin cagily.

"Look, you don't know me, but I've known Bobby for a couple of years and he's a real nice guy. But, take my word for it, there's hardly a girl in town he hasn't been with, me included. As for the tourists, I hate to tell you, but every week it's fresh meat."

"I know you won't believe me, but he was different with me, he really was," croaked Erin.

"Well, it certainly wouldn't be for your singing voice," the blonde girl giggled at Erin. "Okay, joking aside, I am sure he was different, but tell me, how many times have you heard from him since you got home? Once, twice, twenty times. No? Zero? Erin, he does it to everyone. He even has different phones so you can't catch up with him. Honestly sweetie, you have no idea how many girls come back here claiming to be pregnant by him at the end of every season. Hey, he's not the only one, most of the lads are the same; it's just that Bobby is notorious."

Sam caught Carol and Erin exchange glances. "Shit, no. You're not, are you?"

"No, thank goodness," lied Erin, "just been besotted."

"What you need is another holiday to get him out of your system. I'm telling you, it's like riding a bike, well maybe not a bike," the three girls burst out laughing.

Just at that moment, in came her father and uncle Michael. Running to her dad, she threw her arms round his neck.

"Oh, Dad, thank God you're safe. I'm so sorry, so sorry. I never thought for a minute it would turn out like this."

"Hush lassie, don't you worry, everything will be fine. Have you spoken to your mum?"

"Yes, she couldn't really understand me, but I'm sure it'll get better."

For all Paddy was relieved they were fine, Erin especially, they had to get out of Marbella quickly. He had already contacted Ritchie who was on his way. Then there was the blonde girl, the holiday rep.

"What do you think, Michael? She seems kosher and she certainly didn't panic. Give her a few grand. If she's worked here for any length of time, she'll know the score."

"Hey blondie, a word." Michael took the girl onto the balcony, out of view of the others. "You did well tonight. My brother wants me to thank you."

"I'm just glad it turned out okay."

"I'm a bit worried, though. Worried you might have an attack of conscience after we've gone."

"It's none of my business. When I leave this hotel room it's over." Sam was very aware how near the railings she was and how big and menacing Michael looked.

"I want to believe you, but remember, in case you have a change of heart, we're only three hours away."

"You don't have to threaten me, I won't say anything. I live here and I know how to keep myself to myself."

"Good girl," Michael said, handing her a package. "Now on your way and have a safe life."

She couldn't wait to get away. These guys didn't play games. She opened the package and jumped with glee. Fuck it, so what if she'd lost her job? There was enough here to last for a good few years.

And when she ran out, there was always Bobby Mack!

Rewards

"Oh, Erin, it's fab, but I could never afford this. The rent is probably double what I earn in a year. Well, it would be if I ever manage to get another job."

The two girls were viewing a flat just off Byres Road, in an excellent part of the city. A basement flat with a tiny garden at the back, and in the catchment area for all the good nurseries and schools just on the door step. The perfect location for the little family.

Carol and Amy had been staying with the Coyles since their return from Spain. Bridget, Lizzy and even Marie had spoiled the child mercilessly, doing everything in their power to chase away the nightmares. Neither mother nor child had ever known such luxury, but alas, it was time to face reality.

The reality being that she was now unemployed and with no salary, she hadn't been able to keep up her rent on the old place. Not that it was up to much, but it was all she could afford. She couldn't sleep for worrying about her and Amy's future and, kind though it was of Erin to show them round, the girl had no grasp of their situation.

"Never mind if you can afford it or not, do you like it?"

"But I have to mind whether or not I can afford it. Jesus, it would take me years to even get the deposit together. So if you don't mind, I need to go view a couple of other places in Govan."

"You still haven't answered my question. Do you like *this* place?"

"What's not to like? In fact, what's not to love?" Carol answered her wistfully.

"Good, that's settled. Here are the keys. You can move in at the end of the month. I took the liberty of buying it fully furnished, so I hope you like it." Erin grabbed Amy by the hand and raced through to the room she'd already claimed as her bedroom.

"Whoa there, I've just told you I can't afford this, so don't get her hopes up, it's not fair."

"Why not? It's her flat? She's your landlady."

"What the hell are you talking about? My four-year-old daughter can't be my landlady."

"Why can't she?"

"Because she can't."

"That's not an answer. Look, I bought the flat and it's been signed over to Amy. Legally she owns it, but for practical reasons, I maintain guardianship of the property until she's twenty-one. Since there's no rent to pay, why can't you afford it?" said a very smug Erin.

"I'm sorry, we can't take it, Erin. It's far too much. It was a wonderful gesture but we can't accept. Nobody gives away property on this scale."

"We do, and it's all done and dusted, so if you don't move in, it will stay here empty until she's old enough to make her own decisions. Look, Carol, you and she came to my rescue. No hesitation, no questions, well, not many. And you saved my life. But I also put Amy in danger and for that I'll never forgive myself. It was pure luck we got out of that mess. Not only that, because of me you've lost your home and your job. So it's up to the Coyles to make amends."

"A thank you card would have done," laughed Carol.

"I'm not finished. Marie and my gran have been watching you for the past few weeks and they've come up with a proposal."

"Shit. Please, not a pole dancer, I'd close the place down in days."

"Not that, you fool," laughed Erin. "We all think you should go back to hairdressing."

"Really? You know I didn't finish my training before I fell pregnant?"

"So? You could finish your training and start up on your own."

"Why are you crying, Mummy?" asked Amy. "Have you hurt yourself? Shall I kiss it better?"

"I'm fine, sweetie." Carol tousled Amy's curls. "I'm just very happy."

"Silly Mummy. Come and see the swing in my new garden."

"Erin, I don't know what to say."

"Just say YES."

Confessions

"Well, what did she say?" Bridget asked Erin as they were driving to the anti-natal clinic.

"No. For at least the first half dozen times, you know how proud she is, but eventually I persuaded her and she's moving in at the end of the month."

"I'll miss them both," said Bridget. "That Amy's just a little cutie and heaven above, she never stops talking," she smiled. "Speaking of which, when do you next see the consultant? I'm quite worried about your voice, Erin, it seems to be coming and going more and more often and I couldn't bear you to lose it again."

"Don't worry, I've had a word with him and it's all to do with hormones and pregnancy, it'll be fine."

"What about your dad? Has he spoken to you?"

"Nope, he's hardly said a word since we got home. He just can't seem to take this on board."

"I know, love, but I know he'll come round, you just have to give him time. Remember, you were his little princess and he can't abide the thought of you growing up and having a child of your own. What makes it even worse is that the father is Pete McClelland's son. Anybody would be bad, but him, well!"

As his wife and daughter were on their way to the clinic, Paddy and the twins were ensconced in the sitting room at St. Jude's.

"Any news, Paddy?" queried Father Jack.

"No, and I don't expect there to be. There're a couple of things we need to sort out."

Michael placed the holdall on the table and emptied the contents.

"The account books and photographs should be destroyed, they're of no use to any of us, as far as I'm concerned, burn them," Sean put forward. Those at the table nodded.

"There are a number of passports, birth and death certificates. Should we sell them on or destroy?" Once more, Sean posed the questions.

"Destroy them, they're the devils work," said Father Jack. "And I would be happy not knowing the purpose they'd be put to."

"Okay, Father," said the Coyle brothers.

"Now, as to the funds. In bonds and currency there is just over seven hundred and fifty thousand. I propose we make a donation to St. Jude's of two hundred thousand pounds and a further donation to Childline of fifty thousand pounds. Are there any objections?"

Father Jack nodded in agreement; that took care of the roof. St Jude's was an old building and as one part was repaired, another part was falling down. He knew it was filthy, disgusting money, but he also knew if he didn't accept it, someone else would.

"Now to the problem with the drug dealing. What can you tell us, Father? Do you have any information at all because for once, we've drawn a blank."

"I'm sorry, I told you all I knew the last time we spoke. The Irish fly-by-nights were supplementing their income selling drugs, either supplied by Paddy Coyle or for Paddy Coyle, that's all I know."

"So you don't know which, if any, of my lads were involved?"

"No, it could be a misunderstanding. Maybe I got the wrong end of the stick?"

"I don't think so, Father. Usually in these cases there's no smoke without fire. Not to worry, we'll keep a watch, somebody always gets greedy."

"Have you heard anything from the Archbishop about O'Farrell's failure to appear?"

"Not really. The consensus of opinion is that he's been taken ill and not been able to notify us."

"Good," said Paddy. "No hint of anything suspicious?"

"The only good thing about his disappearance is that the sale of candles has doubled. All the old dearies lighting a candle for his return," Father Jack and the Coyle brothers smiled sarcastically.

*

Paddy arrived home before his wife and daughter to an empty house which was most unusual. He wandered around the lounge looking at the framed family pictures, almost every one included Erin at various events; from a baby through to her eighteenth birthday when all this crap had begun.

Right at the back there was even a photo of her first holy communion. So beautiful, so innocent and that was how he'd tried to keep her. But in his mind she was soiled. Nothing could change that, and soiled by McClelland. He knew it was a dreadful way to think of his precious Erin and he was mortally ashamed, but he couldn't help it and he couldn't look at her. And as for the child inside her? If he had his way it would be drowned at birth. He was what he considered to be a good Catholic, but right now Paddy Coyle found no comfort in his church or his family and it was tearing him apart.

Spain

"Maybe he fell overboard from one of those fancy cruise ships?" ventured one of the gypsies.

"He's been in the water a long time, look at his skin."

The old man was burned black from the sun and the salt water. His clothes were torn to shreds and he had only the faintest of pulses.

Hoisting him up onto the dray, the men set off for the monastery, believing the old soul would surely be dead by the time they arrived. Whatever happened, he would not be their responsibility.

For twenty days the monks tended his needs, constantly watching over him. Ministering sips of water and tiny pieces of bread soaked in goat's milk, keeping his blackened skin oiled and supple but with no change in his condition. At around midnight on the twenty first day the stranger made that distinct sound of impending death. The brothers gathered round his bedside to administer the Last Rites and prepare him for his final journey, but they hadn't seen the last of him yet. They were amazed to see the stranger attempt to sit up and open his eyes.

Where was he? He was still alive, they hadn't finished him off yet, he thought as the laughter rattled in his throat. He seemed to have lost his voice. Karma?

Dianne Mack and her son made a formal declaration of missing persons at the Town Hall despite Bobby's pleas to hold off a bit longer. The lad was still convinced that the two would turn up, but his mother was adamant; it was time she faced up to telling Bobby the truth. This was going to be difficult, the boy adored his father and God knows how he would take the news.

Dianne had decided to tell him only what was necessary. There was no need for him to know all the gory details, nor what his father and the canon had actually been involved in. That might have to come later.

"Sit down, Bobby," Dianne spoke as she sat opposite him, holding his hands. "Son, it's time you knew the truth about your father's disappearance and what's been going on."

"When your father and I came to Spain we were on the run from a well-known Glasgow criminal and his family for something your dad was blamed for, but had no hand in."

"Who? And why did he go on the run if he had nothing to do with it?" prompted her son.

"They were the Coyles and nothing would convince them Pete was innocent. Your father and Paddy Coyle were blood brothers. They'd grown up together, served time together and were inseparable. Something happened to do with money. I honestly don't know what, it was a long time ago. Your father swore on your life that he had nothing to do with it and I believed him."

"Anyway, the years went on and there were skirmishes to and fro. Nothing serious until the day of the daughter's Holy Communion. What occurred had nothing to do with the McClellands – again your father had been set up. I've always believed it was one of the twins who were responsible but that's only my opinion. Call it women's intuition, whatever, we had no choice but to leave town, leave everything behind and make a new life from scratch."

"I take it this is the same Erin Coyle I had a fling with at the beginning of the summer?"

"The very same."

"But I told my dad all about it, he said not to worry, there was no way there would be any comeback."

"Well, your dad was wrong. The girl seemingly turned up here a few weeks ago claiming to be pregnant. Unfortunately there was no-one home except Frank, who, for reasons only known to himself, decided to drug her and hold her captive. To make matters even worse, he tried to extort money out of Paddy Coyle for her safe return. Well, as you can imagine, the Coyles arrived here within hours, baying for blood and revenge. By the time I arrived home, it was all over – the bodies had been disposed of and I barely got out of it alive myself. I was warned to keep my mouth shut or they'd come after you. Trust me, Bobby, I know these people and believe me, they don't take prisoners. There was nothing I could do."

Bobby Mack was inconsolable. His father had been his best mate. Up until then he'd clung to the hope that somehow the two men would turn up with some epic tale to tell. Bobby knew Pete was a Jack the lad, but that was what he loved about him and in a way he modelled himself on Pete.

Never in his life had Bobby Mack experienced hurt like he felt now and something inside him, at the core of his being, hardened. From that moment in time he vowed revenge on the Coyles. Beginning with the daughter since it was all her fault; she had started the ball rolling. Stupid enough to believe his happy-ever-after story and now she was pregnant. Well he would take her, the child and everything he could from Paddy Coyle.

An eye for an eye.

The Birth

An uneasy calm had settled on the Coyle household. Bridget and Paddy were civil to one another, but there was none of the jovial banter they'd enjoyed throughout their marriage. No shared excitement at the arrival of their first grandchild. In fact they saw very little of one another these days. They had become the proverbial ships that passed in the night. The prospective granny was in her element preparing for the new baby. If she wasn't shopping for it, she was knitting, if she wasn't knitting, she was poring over magazines with Erin. The nursery was ready and waiting. Everything in the house seemed to revolve round this bloody child, Paddy muttered to himself. It was like the second fucking coming, but not for him.

On the surface, things had gone back to normal fairly quickly after the Spanish ordeal. The trauma Erin had endured was thankfully overshadowed by the return of her voice. Once more she was trailed round physicians and doctors in the hope that now it had returned, it would stay so. Just like before, no-one could give any guarantees. But the *real* elephant in the room was her pregnancy. As far as her father was concerned, it didn't exist. It was never referred to within his earshot. He completely ignored the fact that his daughter was soon to give birth.

Erin had returned to her studies, more as an excuse to get out of the house and away from the atmosphere than for the academic pleasure. However, she seldom socialised with any of her old friends, choosing to spend time with her aunt Marie and Carol, both of whom she felt most comfortable with. As she was nearing her time, she seldom strayed far from home.

She'd tried desperately to regain the relationship she'd once had with Paddy, but he kept his distance and the nearer to her confinement the less time he spent at home, choosing to be at work or Lizzie's instead.

He couldn't wait for it to be all over and then he would put his plan into action. He had decided that as soon as it was possible, he was moving Erin and the brat out. He'd make sure she wanted for nothing, it wasn't some kind of perverse punishment; he just couldn't stand the situation. It was bad enough seeing her everyday, a constant reminder of the past, but to add a McClelland into the mix was too much. His home was no longer his.

Of course, he would get grief from Bridget, that was only to be expected. The girl would surely want her independence, he cited Carol and her youngster as a prime example. He still loved Erin with all his heart, but, try as he might, he could not come to terms with the cuckoo in the nest. As he saw it, this was the only way for his marriage and his family to survive and he prayed that things would eventually change.

No point in staying in bed, she'd been uncomfortable most of the night and had hardly slept a wink. No matter what way she turned, Junior objected. Going downstairs to the kitchen, she found herself alone with Paddy for the first time in weeks.

"Morning," he grunted from behind the newspaper. Never a morning person, this response was not unusual.

"Morning, where's Mum?" she asked him.

"She's gone over to your gran's. She had a fall last night and they're waiting on the doctor."

"Is she okay?"

"Yeah, yeah, it's just precautionary."

"Do you want some breakfast? I'm starving. I feel like I'm eating for three, not two," laughed the girl.

Paddy rose from the table, "No, you're alright, thanks," he replied, leaving the kitchen.

This was ridiculous, Erin thought. When she walked into a room, he walked out. It was as if he couldn't bear the sight of her and she'd had enough. One way or another this was going to stop. Not only did she feel like crap, but with the lack of sleep and hormones all over the place, she couldn't deal with him behaving like a sulky teenager.

"I'm sick and tired of this carry-on, as soon as this baby is born I'm out of here," she yelled at her dad's retreating form. "Did you hear me? I said I'm leaving."

"Yes, I heard you. Why wait? Don't let me stop you, you could be in Spain by lunchtime. I'll give Ritchie a call if you like."

"Spain? Why the fuck would I want to go to Spain?" she yelled back at him.

"To be with your scumbag boyfriend, cos that's what he is, a scumbag. He's hardly been bashing down the door to rescue you or claim you as his woman, has he?"

"I hate you," she shouted at him. "I really, really . . ."

Then silence. Damn, her voice had been breaking up all week and for the moment it had gone. Paddy walked out the front door, slamming it with all his might. She'd never said she hated him before, and she swore at him. His Erin had actually sworn at him. Could she really hate him? Surely not?

He jumped into the car and roared off. Okay, so he'd been told to stay with her until Bridget got back, in case anything happened, but bugger them, this kid had nothing to do with him. What was all that about her voice? Why had it gone again? Maybe the shouting had strained it. Dear God, surely she hadn't lost it again? That would finish him and Bridget; she'd never forgive him if anything else happened to Erin.

It wasn't his fault, she was the one doing all the

shouting, but he had to admit he hadn't helped the situation. Why the fuck had he mentioned Spain? She'd looked quite shocked, obviously he'd hit a nerve. Christ, Bridget would kill him if she came home and he'd deserted his post.

Erin was doubled up with cramps. Jesus, the pain. This couldn't be normal. She crawled on her hands and knees across the kitchen floor and managed to retrieve her phone. Oh, where was everybody? And her bloody voice had given up on her again. Clutching her mobile she dialled her mother, but it went straight to voicemail. Carol. No reply. Of course, she'd be in the salon. No joy from Marie either. She'd be damned if she was going to phone him, not after that performance. But there was something wrong. She heard the crunch of tyres on the gravel. Thank God, she thought as she let out an ear-splitting scream.

By the time the paramedics arrived, the proud grandfather was handing his bawling grandson over to the new mother.

"By God, he's a Coyle alright."

The News

"Senor Bobby, Senor Bobby, phone, phone," called Jose from inside the villa.

"Okay, just a minute. Hello, who's speaking?"

"It's a boy, 7lb 4ozs, born yesterday," the line clicked off.

He walked over to the pool house, "She's had the sprog. A boy."

"Congratulations," whispered the inhabitant.

For a sneak preview of the sequel to
The Silence

THE BETRAYAL

Read on . . .

Happy Families

"This is your Captain speaking. Welcome aboard Flight BA 345 to Malaga. We are now cruising at 50,000ft and the outside temperature is minus 40 deg. Our estimated time of arrival is 12.08 . . ."

It seemed a lifetime ago since the passengers in seats 1A, B and C had last heard that announcement and dear God, how all their lives had changed over the past year. For starters, Erin had no fear that her father would storm the plane and carry her off. No, that fear was long gone. Mainly because she and Paddy were again not on speaking terms. He was furious that not only was she taking his six-month-old grandchild out of the country, but that she was entering that den of vipers. His parting shot that morning as she left for the airport had been:

"Don't coming running back to me when this all goes tits up. You've made your bed, lady. Shame you've already lain in it."

"Oh, piss off, Dad and give it a rest. I'm only going

for a couple of weeks and it's only fair they should get to know the baby. Whether or not you like it, he is as much a McClelland as he is a Coyle."

The slamming of the door shook the whole house.

As usual her mother didn't say a word, but Erin knew she was the one who ruled the roost and would calm her dad down.

"God, I can't believe we're on our way back," said her companion nervously. "Are you sure you're doing the right thing?"

"It's a bit late now, we can hardly get off at the next stop," Erin laughed. "Look, if it all goes belly up, we'll take the next flight home, it's that simple."

Carol wasn't quite so confident about the reception they would receive in Spain, but once again she was here to cover Erin's back and give her moral support. Whatever happened, she reasoned it couldn't top their last visit. Christ. Murder, kidnapping and fleeing the country. Not exactly a Thomson's week in the sun.

"Hey, listen, I'm not taking shit from either of them, especially the mother. She insisted she wanted to get to know her grandson, so she better play ball with me. This time I'm calling the shots."

"Are you sure? Do you think Bobby will be okay? Remember, he's back on his own turf and you don't have the infamous Paddy Coyle standing right behind you."

"I know, but Paddy Coyle is only three hours away and Bobby is well aware of that."

"True, but you better hope he doesn't find out the situation between you and Paddy."

"Don't worry, my dad will be fine. Going a few days without seeing his precious grandson will soon have him begging for forgiveness. Anyway, Mum won't let it go on, not after what happened the last time."

"Well, I hope you're right! What sort of reception can we expect? Do they know we're arriving today?" Carol asked her.

"No, they know I'm coming sometime this week, but not exactly when. It sounds a bit weird but I wanted to be in control from the start, so we'll get the kids settled and have a bit of us-time before entering the lion's den."

"Don't say things like that," shivered Carol. "I can't stop thinking about the last trip."

"Me too, but remember, neither Bobby or his mother had anything to do with what went on before."

"I'm not so sure. I wouldn't trust either of them as far as I could throw them," replied Carol.

"That's one of the reasons I've kept it low key. They'll only know we're here when I choose to tell them. Stop worrying, we'll have a nice couple of days, top up the tan, and then . . ."

At that precise moment a stewardess approached them carrying an ice bucket containing a bottle of champagne and a couple of glasses.

"Miss Coyle?"

"Yeah," answered Erin.

"Champagne, compliments of Mr Bobby Mack."

The woman expertly opened the bottle, poured out two glasses and handed them to the surprised passengers.

"They don't know when we're arriving?" Carol sneered! " Don't know what flight we are on?"

"What can I say?" a dumbstruck Erin replied.

"And you think you're in control? It's *you* calling the shots? Oh, it looks like it. And what does the card say?" She grabbed the small note before her friend could.

"'Can't wait to see you, meet you at three, everything taken care of, Love Bobby.' Well, so much for the 'us time'," Carol laughed. "Seriously, you need to be very careful. This guy has a lot of pull here. I just don't trust him at all."

Despite her friend's warning, Erin was secretly delighted. There was no way she was going to fall for Bobby the way she had before, but he *was* the father of her baby and of course she had 'happy ever after dreams', but she wouldn't be taken in a second time, she had her son to consider.

Titles by the Same Author

Life Behind Bars: Confessions of a Pub Landlady

Life on the Outside: The Lunatics have taken over the Asylum

Life in the Fat Lane: Chocolate after Midnight doesn't Count